W9-BSB-190

KITTEN in the CANDY CORN

Ben M. Baglio

Illustrations by Ann Baum

Cover illustration by
Mary Ann Lasher

AN
APPLE
PAPERBACK

SCHOLASTIC INC.
New York Toronto London Auckland Sydney
Mexico City New Delhi Hong Kong Buenos Aires

Special thanks to Lucy Courtenay

Thanks also to C. J. Hall, B. Vet. Med., M.R.C.V.S., for reviewing the veterinary information contained in this book.

If you purchased this book without a cover, you should be aware that this book is stolen property. It was reported as "unsold and destroyed" to the publisher, and neither the author nor the publisher has received any payment for this "stripped book."

No part of this publication may be reproduced in whole or in part, or stored in a retrieval system, or transmitted in any form or by any means, electronic, mechanical, photocopying, recording, or otherwise, without written permission of the publisher. For information regarding permission, write to Working Partners Limited, 1 Albion Place, London W6 0QT, United Kingdom.

ISBN 0-439-68758-6

Text copyright © 2004 by Working Partners Limited.
Created by Working Partners Limited, London W6 0QT, United Kingdom.
Illustrations copyright © 2004 by Ann Baum.

All rights reserved. Published by Scholastic Inc., 557 Broadway, New York, NY 10012, by arrangement with Working Partners Limited. ANIMAL ARK is a trademark of Working Partners Limited. SCHOLASTIC, APPLE PAPERBACKS, and associated logos are trademarks and/or registered trademarks of Scholastic Inc.

12 11 10 9 8   6 7 8 9/0

Printed in the U.S.A.   40
First Scholastic printing, October 2004

One

"Well, what do you think?" Mandy Hope demanded. She held up a cardboard cat mask. It was painted black and had sharp ears. Its long white whiskers were made from pipe cleaners. "It's taken me ages to stick the whiskers on. I'll wear a black sweatshirt top and leggings as well, and Gran's making me a belt with a tail."

Mandy's best friend, James Hunter, looked up from his piece of buttered toast. He squinted in the bright morning sun that was slanting through the Hopes' kitchen window. "It's great," he said, impressed. "You'll make my costume look really boring."

"I'm glad I invited you over for breakfast now!"

1

Mandy joked. It was Tuesday morning, the second official day of their vacation, and she and James had planned an early start to make the most of their week off. Most important of all, they had a Halloween party to plan. They were going to hold it at the end of the week. "You'll look fantastic as Harry Potter, James," Mandy continued, remembering what he had told her about his costume. "Everyone will know who you are. Do you think they'll realize I'm Catwoman?"

"Catwoman!" Emily Hope, Mandy's mother, swung around from pouring herself a cup of coffee and clapped one hand to her forehead. "Of course! We've been scratching our heads all weekend about your Halloween costume."

"Come on, Mom," Mandy teased. "Since when have I ever dressed up as anything but some kind of animal for Halloween?"

Dr. Emily laughed. Everyone knew that Mandy was animal crazy. Her parents ran Animal Ark, the veterinary clinic in the town of Welford in Yorkshire, and Mandy loved every hectic second of it. Whatever the problem, whatever kind of animal, she was always eager to help.

Her dad, Dr. Adam, looked up from a list he was making at the other end of the table. "What about last year, Mandy? That wasn't an animal costume, was it?"

"Of course it was, Dad!" Mandy was indignant. "OK,

so I got the tail wrong, but everyone knew I was a squirrel."

"With the straightest, dangliest tail ever to decorate a squirrel," said Dr. Adam solemnly.

Mandy made a face at her dad, then reached for another piece of toast. "I can't wait for Saturday," she said, and sighed. She turned to James. "Is Blackie going to wear a costume this year?"

James's black Labrador had been sniffing under the table for crumbs. He stopped and pricked up his ears when he heard his name.

"I thought maybe a bat," said James, rubbing his glasses on the bottom of his sweatshirt. "He's the right color and everything, and his ears would be a great shape if I could figure out how to stop them from flopping over."

"We can't possibly let Blackie join in," said Dr. Adam, shaking his head. "Those sharp canines of his would give him too much of an advantage in the apple bobbing."

Mandy and James exchanged a grin at the thought of Blackie with his head in the washtub, chasing apples.

"Come on, you two," said Dr. Adam, rapping the table with his pencil. "I'm stuck here. We're supposed to be making a list of party games, and I only have bobbing for apples so far. The clinic opens in fifteen minutes. Brainstorm time!"

"Identifying slimy things in jars," James said promptly, peering over Dr. Adam's shoulder at the list. "That's always a good one. Peeled grapes, spaghetti, jelly — stuff like that. It's really gross when you put your hand in and have to guess what you're feeling."

"How about fishing jelly beans out of flour with your teeth?" Mandy suggested.

"Powdered sugar would taste nicer," Mandy's mom pointed out, placing the breakfast plates in the dishwasher.

Maybe it was the excitement of knowing that the Halloween party was only four days away, but the ideas suddenly came thick and fast. Eating chocolate with chopsticks. Halloween Pictionary. Pin the hat on the headless horseman.

"What about doughnuts on strings?" James suggested enthusiastically. "Cookies, too."

"Don't mention doughnuts and cookies." Dr. Adam groaned, putting his hand on his stomach. "I feel hungry just thinking about them."

"Dad's on another diet," Mandy explained to James. "Mom insisted. He's getting a bit of a stomach."

"Just enough to make me cuddly," Dr. Adam protested. "What I wouldn't do for a cookie right now!"

As Dr. Emily flapped a dish towel at him, there was a

quiet knock at the kitchen door. There was only one person Mandy knew who knocked as politely as that.

"I bet that's John!" she said, getting out of her chair and running to open the door.

John Hardy lived with his father and stepmother at the Fox and Goose in Welford. He was away at school for much of the year, but he was good friends with Mandy and James and saw them whenever he came home for vacation. Mandy enjoyed spending time with him and his rabbits, Brandy and Bertie. They got along so well that sometimes she found it hard to believe John didn't live in Welford all year-round.

Mandy opened the door and beamed at the boy who was standing there. He had neatly brushed brown hair and clean, ironed jeans, and he was shifting from one foot to the other as if he was trying to make up his mind about coming in.

"Hello, John!" Mandy exclaimed. "We were expecting to see you yesterday. Didn't you get out on Friday, like us?"

"We got out on Sunday, actually," said John. "Sorry I didn't come over before now. I've been sort of busy."

"Playing with Brandy and Bertie, right?" asked Mandy. "It must be nice to see them again." A little girl in town named Imogen Parker Smythe looked after

John's rabbits while he was away at school, and Mandy knew that John missed them a lot.

John's solemn face lit up. "It was great," he agreed. "Imogen has looked after them really well. They're much bigger. I came over to see if you have any of those chewy sticks for them, for cleaning their teeth."

"I'm sure we'll find some for you, John," said Mandy's mom. "Come in. I think these three could use your help."

John carefully stepped over Blackie, took off his coat, and hung it neatly by the back door. "What are you doing?" he asked.

"Thinking of Halloween games for the party," James replied.

John looked surprised. "What party?"

"Our annual Halloween party," Mandy explained, picking up her cat mask and waving it with a flourish. "It's a costume party, and it's on Saturday. Can you come?"

"And do you know any good party games?" James added.

John looked delighted. "I'd love to come," he said. Leaning over, he studied the list of games with the air of a botanist studying a rare plant. "What's this one?" he said, pointing at James's suggestion of cookies on strings.

"Dad's favorite," said Mandy. "You hang doughnuts

and cookies from the ceiling on pieces of string, and you have to eat them without using your hands."

John's eyebrows shot up. "Don't you get very messy?" he said cautiously.

"Very," Mandy agreed. "It's great."

John frowned. "How does it work?"

Dr. Adam clapped his hands. "It seems we need a demonstration!" he said with a gleam in his eye.

"Dad," Mandy said warningly, "don't forget your diet!"

Dr. Adam produced some string and reached for the cookie jar. "We all need to make sacrifices in the name of research," he said, picking up the lid and removing two fat, crumbly chocolate chip cookies. "Mandy, James, tie these two for me, would you? Then we have to hang them from something."

"I'll hold them," Mandy offered. She hopped up on a kitchen chair and held out her hands for the cookie strings.

"Hold them up high," Dr. Adam advised. "We've got to be on tiptoe for this. Now, on your mark, get set, GO!"

Mandy got a terrible attack of the giggles as her dad gobbled down the first cookie at lightning speed. Then he and James dueled over the second cookie, with James having to jump up really high to compete. Breathless with laughter, they soon had cookie crumbs all over their faces and clothes. Blackie ran back and

forth, gobbling up the cookie crumbs that littered the floor.

"So much for the diet, Adam," said Dr. Emily, sighing.

"What do you think of the game, John?" Mandy asked once she'd gotten her breath back.

John grinned. "Excellent!"

Dr. Adam looked at his watch. "We just have time to take a look at the guest list. You are in charge of making the invitations, Mandy, OK? They have to go out by Thursday or no one will know about it in time. So who do we invite?"

"Mom, Dad, me, Gran and Grandpa, James, Blackie, and John. That makes" — Mandy counted on her fingers — "eight."

"What about trick-or-treating?" Mandy's mom wanted to know. "Who are you going to visit?"

"Ernie Bell usually likes to see our costumes," Mandy said. "And Walter Pickard —"

"He's just arrived with Flicker," came the voice of Jean Knox, the Animal Ark receptionist, who was standing at the door to the waiting room. "He says he has the first appointment this morning. Of course, I can't find the appointment book anywhere, so we'll just have to hope that he's right, won't we?" She sighed and disappeared back into the clinic without waiting for a reply.

"Hey, wasn't that weird!" said Mandy after a moment. "Just when I said Walter's name."

John leaned forward. "That's Halloween for you," he said seriously. "Expect the unexpected!"

Walter smiled broadly when Mandy, James, and John came into the clinic waiting room. "Hello there," he said. "On vacation, I take it?"

"Yup," Mandy replied. "Is Flicker all right?"

Walter looked down at the cat basket by his feet. "Not really. She's got a nasty cough," he answered.

"We have another cat in for observation with the same thing," said Mandy sympathetically. "I think there's a bug going around."

A quiet cough floated up from the basket. Mandy knelt down to see Flicker curled at the very back of the basket, staring up at her with wide, fearful eyes.

"Hello, sweetheart," she said softly. She looked up at Walter. "May I pick her up?"

"Of course you may," Walter nodded. "Got to get her out of her basket sometime. But it won't be easy. You know how she can be when she's scared."

The little cat flinched into the corner of the basket as Mandy reached in and petted her fine black ears, talking soothingly all the time. Gradually, Flicker began to re-

lax, though her green eyes remained wide and distrust-
ful. After a moment or two, Mandy moved her hand
around to tickle the cat's chin. When she finally
scooped the cat out of her basket, Flicker was still and
relaxed. A gentle rumbling sound came from deep in
her throat, and she rested her neat black-and-white
head in the crook of Mandy's neck.

Walter shook his head in amazement. "You've got
quite a touch there, Mandy."

Mandy grinned at Walter. "All part of the Animal Ark
service."

Walter scratched the little cat between her ears. "She
still remembers you," he said. "She knows if it weren't
for you, she probably wouldn't be alive."

"Mandy rescued Flicker when Welford had those bad
floods," James explained to John. "The poor thing
floated right up to the door in a barrel! She was washed
away from the farm where she lived when the river
burst its banks."

Dr. Emily came over. "Let's take a look at this cough
then, young Flicker," she said with a smile. "Mandy,
could you bring her into the examining room for me?"

Mandy carried Flicker into the examining room,
closely followed by Walter. Dr. Emily examined the cat
swiftly and gently, looking down her throat with a small

flashlight and listening to her chest with a stethoscope. The cat mewed plaintively, and Walter petted her with one huge finger.

"Is it the same thing that Misty has?" Mandy wanted to know. Misty was the cat in the residential unit.

"I think so," Dr. Emily replied, washing her hands. "We've caught it earlier in this case, though, so she doesn't need to stay here. I have some cough medicine you can give her, Walter, twice a day. Just keep her warm, and she'll be good as new in a few days."

"Is chocolate the latest hair accessory?" Walter suddenly asked Mandy as they returned to the waiting room. He pulled a chocolate chip from Mandy's hair.

Mandy laughed. "Nope!"

Sitting on one of the waiting room chairs, James looked up from the wildlife magazine he was reading. "We were practicing one of the games we're having at the party on Saturday," he explained.

"I love Halloween," Walter said, setting Flicker back into her basket. "There's something about the dark evenings and autumn leaves and the bare tree trunks — all black and orange and Halloweenlike. Do you know what I mean?"

Mandy nodded.

"Did you have Halloween parties when you were young, Mr. Pickard?" John wanted to know.

"We certainly did," Walter said. "Apple bobbing, pumpkin carving, all that stuff."

"I've carved a pumpkin this year," Mandy said proudly. "It's on the kitchen windowsill. It looks really spooky when I put a candle inside it. Mom made some soup with the insides on Sunday."

"We used to have pumpkin-carving competitions in town," Walter went on, "until one year, the minister banned it. Someone's goat got into his garden and ate the prize pumpkin he'd been growing especially for the competition."

"A goat in the minister's garden? Sounds like a bit of early trick-or-treating," James suggested.

Mandy leaned forward. "It was you, wasn't it? Who let the goat in? Come on, Walter, you can tell us."

Walter laughed. "That's for me to know!" he said. "Anyway, it was harmless enough. Not like some of the tricks they pull these days. You won't be playing any silly pranks this year, will you? The town has enough to worry about at the moment."

Mandy frowned. "What do you mean?"

"Haven't you heard?" asked Walter, surprised.

"Heard what?"

Flicker mewed and scratched at the side of her basket, and Walter reached down to reassure her. "I'd better be getting this young lady home," he said, picking up the basket. "I'm sure you'll hear all about it before long."

Mandy reached through the basket opening with her finger and tickled Flicker's neck. She loved all the animals who came to the clinic, but the little black-and-white cat had a special place in her heart. Not for the first time, Mandy wished that she had a cat of her own.

Maybe that's why I'm dressing up as Catwoman this year, she thought with a sigh. *It's the closest I'm going to get to the real thing.*

Two

Because the sun was shining, Mandy, John, and James decided to walk into town with Walter and Flicker. It wasn't long before they were strolling down the narrow road, Blackie leaping at the end of his leash, John clutching a handful of chewing sticks for his rabbits, and Walter carrying Flicker as carefully as if she were a carton of eggs. As they approached the town crossroads, a cold breeze tugged at Mandy's coat, making it flap and startling Blackie into a volley of barking.

"Don't frighten Flicker, Blackie," Mandy scolded. "She's had a bad morning already."

Blackie whined and retreated behind James's legs, staring suspiciously at Mandy's coat.

"I think Blackie's more scared than Flicker," Walter observed. "Ah, here we are. So I'll see you on Saturday night for trick-or-treating?"

"Will you have some candy, Mr. Pickard?" John asked hopefully.

"You'll have to wait and see," Walter said and grinned.

Mandy, James, and John waved at the elderly man as he made his way down the path beside the Fox and Goose to his tiny white house, which nestled behind the restaurant.

"Tom will be pleased to see Flicker back home," Mandy said. Tom was Walter's other cat, a big black-and-white cat. He was famous for his bad temper, but he had grown very fond of Flicker after his other friend, Scraps, had to be put down.

"Sara will be pleased to see *me* back home," John remarked, looking at his watch. "I promised I wouldn't be too long, and it's already nine-thirty. I haven't fed the rabbits yet."

"Don't worry, I have," said a voice from behind them.

They turned to see Sara Hardy, John's stepmother, getting to her feet. She was holding some broken pottery pieces that Mandy recognized as part of a flowerpot that usually stood outside the door of the restaurant.

"Don't look so worried, John." Sara smiled. "I thought Mandy would keep you for a while."

"What happened to your flowerpot, Mrs. Hardy?" Mandy asked curiously.

"This?" Sara asked, holding up one of the pieces. "Heaven only knows. The wind must have knocked it over. It's been pretty blustery today."

Blackie was sniffing around the flowerpot pieces that were still lying on the ground.

"Hey! Look at his fur," James said suddenly.

On the way to town, Blackie's fur had been blown in all directions by the wind. Now it lay sleek and neat against his skin.

Mandy guessed at once what James meant. "The wind couldn't have blown over the flowerpot," she said with a frown. "It's too sheltered by the door. I wonder what really happened."

Sara sighed and looked down at the mess of pottery, dirt, and flowers at her feet. "All I know is that this is going to take a while to clean up. I don't suppose you could lend a hand, could you?"

With four pairs of hands (plus a less helpful four paws and a tail), the cleanup took less than five minutes. Soon, Mandy, James, and Blackie were on their way back to Animal Ark, having promised to come over later and see the rabbits using their new toothbrushes.

"Don't you think it's odd?" Mandy said as they walked back to the clinic.

"What?" asked James, busily tugging Blackie away from an interesting smell at the side of the road.

"That business with the flowerpot and the wind." Mandy stopped for a moment. "If the wind didn't blow it over, it must have been something else — or some-*one* else."

"Who'd knock over a flowerpot?" James asked.

"Someone with nothing better to do," Mandy replied thoughtfully. She thought back to the interrupted conversation she'd had with Walter, about there being some kind of trouble in the town.

Blackie gave a sharp bark, interrupting Mandy's train of thought. She looked up. "James!" she said, entranced. "Look at that beautiful dog!"

About fifty yards farther down the road, a red-haired boy was coming around the corner with a golden retriever. The dog's long fur rippled like barley in the wind, and its ears pricked up when it saw Blackie. The boy was fiddling with the zipper on his jacket, so he hadn't seen Mandy or James.

"It's Matt Burness," James said. His voice was strangely flat. "I wondered when we'd be seeing him."

"Who?" Mandy asked, her eyes fixed on the retriever.

"A boy at school. He's just moved to town. Come on."

To Mandy's surprise, James tugged at Blackie's leash and started walking hurriedly in the opposite direction.

Mandy was confused. "What's the matter?" she asked, breaking into a trot to keep up with her friend. "Don't you like him?"

James shrugged and kept walking. "What's to like?" he said. "He's a bully. He always hangs around with these tough guys who act like they rule my class. He's just moved from Walton to Welford. I've heard his pals teasing him about being a country bumpkin and having no friends here. Well, big deal! I'm not going to talk to him."

Mandy put out a hand and caught James's arm, slowing him down. "We could try being friendly," she insisted. "If he's just moved to town, he may be lonely."

James snorted. "Trust me, Mandy," he said. "He's trouble."

Mandy stood in the middle of the road, undecided. The boy didn't look too bad. His red hair fell almost to his shoulders, and he wore baggy jeans and a green baseball cap with the brim slanting to one side. And she really wanted to meet his dog. What should she do?

Blackie made the decision for her by pulling free from James and bounding up the road, his tail wagging joyfully. The boy looked up to see the black Labrador racing toward him and gave a half smile. But when he

noticed Mandy and James, the smile was replaced by a sullen frown.

James stayed well back, but Mandy followed Blackie. "Hello," she said when she came up to the boy. She looked down at Blackie, who was frisking around the retriever as if they were the best of friends. "You have the most beautiful dog," she said in a rush. "What's his name?"

There was a brief silence, and for a moment Mandy thought that the boy wasn't going to say anything at all.

"Biscuit," he muttered at last. "Because of his color."

Mandy crouched down in front of the retriever and held out her arms. "Hello, Biscuit," she whispered. "You're gorgeous, aren't you?"

Biscuit grinned at her, his long pink tongue lolling out of his mouth.

"I'm Mandy," she said, standing up again and smiling at the boy. "You're new in the town, aren't you?"

The boy said nothing and fiddled with Biscuit's leash.

"It's just that I've never seen you before, and I'd remember you," Mandy continued. "And I'd definitely remember Biscuit."

"That's small-town life for you," the boy said scornfully. "Everyone knows everyone." He jerked his head in James's direction. "I'm sure he's told you all about me, so there's no need to act like you want to be my friend. I don't want to be here, so just leave me alone, OK?"

He tugged sharply at the retriever's leash. "Come on, Biscuit. Let's go home."

Mandy felt puzzled and hurt as the boy walked down the road with his shoulders hunched, past the crossroads and out of sight.

"Told you," said James, walking up to her.

"And you're always right, I suppose," said Mandy, still staring after the boy.

"In this case, yes," James said firmly. "Come on. Let's get back."

James tied Blackie in a sheltered spot outside the clinic when they got back to Animal Ark, in case there were any small animals inside. The waiting room had filled up since they had left. Mrs. Parker Smythe was sitting in one corner with her daughter Imogen's rabbit, Button, on her lap. John's rabbits had come from one of Button's litters, and Imogen was the girl who looked after Brandy and Bertie when John was away at school.

"Hello, Mrs. Parker Smythe. What's the matter with Button?" James asked.

Mrs. Parker Smythe was a tall, elegant woman with shining blond hair pinned into a French twist on the back of her head. She petted Button and indicated a small nick on one of her ears. "Button had a little accident with a piece of loose wire in her cage," she explained in her light, silvery voice. "Darling Immi was far too upset to come with me today. It's been simply dreadful for her."

Button, who seemed fairly cheerful, shook his head and butted James's outstretched fingers as if to say hello.

A loud, bossy voice drew Mandy's attention to the reception desk, where another of her mom and dad's clients, Mrs. Ponsonby, was talking to Jean. Pandora, Mrs. Ponsonby's spoiled Pekingese, was lying on the floor by her owner's feet with her head between her paws.

". . . terrible pain," Mrs. Ponsonby was saying. "We really must see the vet immediately."

"I'm sorry, Mrs. Ponsonby," Jean said apologetically, "but we're very busy today, as you can see. You will have to wait your turn, I'm afraid. If you'll just take a seat, Dr. Emily will see Pandora as soon as she can."

Mrs. Ponsonby heaved a sigh and settled her blue-rimmed spectacles a little straighter on the end of her nose. "But Pandora can't *walk*," she said, her bottom lip wobbling. "This toenail is causing her the most dreadful agony. It's terribly cruel —"

"Hello, Mrs. Ponsonby," Mandy broke in cheerfully,

bending down to scratch Pandora in the spot she liked best, right between her shoulders. Pandora gave a whine of pleasure and wriggled under Mandy's hand.

"Ah, Mandy." Mrs. Ponsonby turned toward her, beaming. "Pandora's always pleased to see you, aren't you, my darling little girl?" She puckered her fuchsia lips at the Peke and made kissing noises. "You have such a way with animals, dear," she told Mandy, scooping Pandora up and tucking the little Peke under her arm.

Mandy led Mrs. Ponsonby to a seat by the waiting room window, not far from Mrs. Parker Smythe and Button. Jean gave her a grateful glance and turned to answer the phone.

"You will follow in your parents' footsteps here at Animal Ark, won't you?" Mrs. Ponsonby asked Mandy, settling herself in a chair and placing Pandora on her lap. "I can't imagine anyone else looking after my treasures. You simply can't trust strangers these days."

Mrs. Parker Smythe looked up. "You are quite right, Mrs. Ponsonby," she said earnestly. "Have you heard about those dreadful vandals in town?" She lowered her voice. "Strangers, of course."

"Vandals?" Mandy echoed. "Here in Welford?"

"Oh, yes!" Mrs. Parker Smythe exclaimed. "The worst kind. Scribbling graffiti in the town phone booth and hanging around the restaurant, though goodness knows why, because they're far too young to go in there alone."

The broken flowerpot, Mandy thought suddenly.

"I've seen one of them, I'm sure of it," Mrs. Ponsonby chipped in importantly. "A ruffian if ever there was one. Red hair down to his shoulders! They say you have to watch the red-haired ones. They have such terrible tempers."

"We're not all bad," said Dr. Emily with a grin, standing at the door of the examining room and twirling the end of her dark red ponytail around her finger. "Provided you don't feed us after midnight. Now, who's next?"

Mrs. Ponsonby blushed and bent down to fiddle with Pandora's collar. As Mrs. Parker Smythe carried Button across to the examining room, Mandy glanced across at James, whose eyebrows had shot up under his hair. Mrs. Ponsonby's description fitted Matt Burness almost exactly. It seemed that James was right after all.

Matt was trouble with a capital *T*.

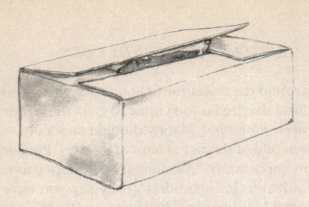

Three

Halfway to the examining room, Mrs. Parker Smythe suddenly stopped dead in her tracks and looked out the window. "Who on earth is that?" she asked.

Mandy and James both ran to see. Coming up the Animal Ark driveway, with a large cardboard box tucked under one arm, was the most extraordinary-looking person Mandy had ever seen. The tall woman had iron gray hair in a long braid that hung down from beneath the brim of a battered black hat, and she was draped from top to toe in an enormous black cape. Each of her long strides made the cape billow out to reveal a pair of red-and-black-striped tights that ended in two sturdy black lace-up boots.

"It's *her*!" Mrs. Ponsonby said and gasped, peering over Mandy's shoulder. "Araminta Greenwood. I haven't seen her in town for a while. Whatever does she have in that box?"

Araminta Greenwood. The name sounded familiar to Mandy. Where had she heard it before?

"I've heard people talk about her," James whispered dramatically, his eyes wide and a little fearful. "They say that she's a *witch*."

Araminta Greenwood certainly looked the part. The only thing missing was a broomstick. Mrs. Parker Smythe looked a little frightened and hurried into the examining room with Button.

It was coming back to Mandy now. "She's the woman who treats wild animals in the woods!" she said in excitement. "Mom and Dad told me she set a doe's broken leg once, and it healed as good as new." Her heart began to pound with expectation. "She must have a wild animal in that box. Maybe a rabbit? Or a fox cub?" She hoped the animal hadn't been hurt by a snare or a trap. It was always horrible to see an injured wild animal, but even worse when its injuries had been caused by humans.

James pushed his glasses up on his nose. "The box

looks too big for a rabbit or a fox cub," he said. "Maybe there's a full-grown fox in there. Or maybe," he whispered, "it's her — what do you call it? — you know, the animals that witches have to help with their spells?"

"Familiar," Mandy said absently.

"Exactly," said James. "Her familiar. Maybe one of her spells went wrong and she turned her cat into a toad or something!"

Somehow it wasn't difficult to picture Araminta Greenwood stirring a cauldron and muttering magic words with a black cat or a toad by her side.

Mandy grinned. "I can't see Mom or Dad being able to solve a problem like that," she said. "I think your first idea was better, James. A full-grown fox."

James didn't look convinced. "I'd better go and see if Blackie's OK," he muttered.

"Ms. Greenwood isn't going to turn Blackie into a puff of smoke!" Mandy exclaimed.

"You can't be too sure," James replied darkly, and hurried outside.

"She lives alone in the woods near Bleakfell Hall," Mrs. Ponsonby told Mandy with a theatrical shiver. "I've heard the most extraordinary noises coming from her house when I've been walking my darlings in the woods. I wouldn't be at all surprised to learn that what they say about her is true. After all, where there's smoke . . ."

The half-finished sentence was left hanging in the air as the door opened and Araminta Greenwood swept in on a draft of chilly October air. Up close, she looked even taller, and her cape seemed to fill the whole room in a swirl of black. Mrs. Ponsonby shrank back against her seat and pulled Pandora closer to her. Ignoring the curious glances, Araminta Greenwood walked straight over to the reception desk and put the box down.

"May I help you?" Jean asked politely.

"Badger," Araminta Greenwood said. She had an odd, abrupt way of speaking as if she were unused to conversations and wanted to use the fewest words possible. "Injured. Can't fix him on my own."

As she spoke, she opened up the flaps on the top of the box.

Mandy caught her breath as a pointed black-and-white snout appeared, warily sniffing the air. "How wonderful!" she said, and gasped.

Araminta Greenwood looked around. "Not so wonderful for the badger," she said drily.

Mandy went over to the reception desk and gazed into the box. The badger was shifting restlessly from side to side, hampered by a thick woolen blanket that Ms. Greenwood had wrapped around him. He gave a few deep, unhappy growls and sniffed the air again. He looked young but fully grown. Mandy guessed that he was searching for the cool, woody smells of his forest home; the antiseptic smell of the clinic must have seemed very strange and frightening.

"Poor thing!" she exclaimed. "What happened?"

"He fell," said Araminta Greenwood. "There's a steep bank near the house. Seen him hunting there a few times. Went out this morning, and he was lying at the bottom. Poor creature tried to get away from me, but that leg stopped him."

"What do you think he was hunting?" Mandy asked.

"Worms." Araminta Greenwood gave a glimmer of a smile. "Rather him than me."

Mandy grinned. Even if the woman *was* a witch, she had a good sense of humor.

Just then, Dr. Emily stepped out of the examining room with Mrs. Parker Smythe. Button had a neat white dressing on her ear and was flicking her head in annoyance, trying to dislodge the offending bandage.

"Just keep that ear clean, and the cut will heal," Mandy's mom said, ushering Mrs. Parker Smythe through the waiting room and toward the door. "And tell Imogen not to worry. Button is going to be fine."

She glanced across at the reception desk. "Hello, Ms. Greenwood," she said with a smile, walking forward and holding out her hand for the woman to shake. "What brings you here?"

"It's a badger, Mom." Mandy's words tumbled out in her eagerness to explain. "He's hurt his leg."

"This is my daughter, Mandy," Dr. Emily explained. "She often helps in the clinic."

Araminta Greenwood smiled at Mandy. "Chip off the old block, I see," she said. "Interested in animals, are you?"

"Crazy about them," Mandy agreed. "Especially wild animals. Did you really mend a doe's leg?"

Araminta Greenwood looked surprised. "Where did you hear that?"

"Come along," Dr. Emily said hurriedly. "Mandy, can you give me a hand? Simon's busy in the residential unit at the moment."

"Ahem!" Mrs. Ponsonby cleared her throat and cautiously glanced at Araminta Greenwood. "I believe I was next, Dr. Emily. Pandora is in a *great* deal of discomfort."

"Adam!" Dr. Emily called to the kitchen. "Can you see Mrs. Ponsonby and Pandora for me?"

Mandy's dad appeared, holding a cup of coffee in one hand and shrugging his white coat on with the other, and swept Mrs. Ponsonby into the second examining room. A crumb of chocolate chip cookie was clinging to his chin. Mandy rolled her eyes at her dad's lack of willpower, before following her mom and Ms. Greenwood. She put on her white coat and washed her hands at the sink in the corner of the examining room, then turned to see what her mom needed her to do.

"I wrapped him in a blanket to stop him from scratching me," Ms. Greenwood said. "He's strong as an ox, and not very happy."

The badger growled again and shuffled around, trying to free himself from the folds of the blanket.

"I can see that," Dr. Emily replied. "Mandy, could you pass me the gloves?"

Mandy handed over a pair of heavy-duty gloves. Her mom carefully lifted the protesting badger from his box, speaking reassuringly to him as she unwrapped the blanket and set the animal down on the table. The badger kept up his warning growl, and Mandy felt sure he had very sharp teeth.

Simon, the veterinary nurse, poked his head around the door. "Do you need me, Dr. Emily?" he asked. "I've finished in the residential unit. Jean said something about a wild animal."

"Perfect timing," said Dr. Emily, putting the blanket to one side and holding the badger down with her other hand. "Meet Brock the badger. We'll have to sedate him to get a good look at that leg."

Sedating an animal was a tricky job and too specialized for Mandy. She helped Simon wheel out the gas

tank, and he fitted the mask to the badger's snout. Soon
the only noise to be heard was the quiet hiss of the gas
and the badger's gentle breathing.

"OK," said Dr. Emily. "Let's take a good look at him
now."

The badger seemed oddly bigger when he was asleep.
Mandy figured he was almost a yard long from his snout
to the tip of his tail. There was something bearlike about
him, with his broad, brindled back and short legs. His tail
was very short, and his claws looked wickedly sharp.

Araminta Greenwood leaned over Dr. Emily's shoulder. "The bone isn't too badly displaced from what I could see, but old Brock is having trouble putting his weight on it. Hairline fracture, perhaps?"

"Why do you all call him Brock?" Mandy wanted to know.

"It's the old country word for badger," Dr. Emily explained, gently palpating the wild animal's leg. "I agree with you, Ms. Greenwood. We'll need to splint that leg for about three weeks. How are you doing with the anesthetic, Simon?"

"Fine," said Simon. "Go ahead."

Dr. Emily looked across at Mandy. "Get me some orthoboard, would you, dear? It's over there, second drawer down." The clinic often used orthoboard to splint broken limbs instead of the more traditional plaster cast. It was easy to apply and only took five minutes to set.

Mandy took a piece of orthoboard from the drawer. It looked like a sheet of thin brown cardboard. She put it in some hot water for a minute to soften it, then passed it to her mom, who measured it against the sleeping badger. Mandy helped to cut it to the right size before her mother tucked it underneath the badger's foreleg and wrapped it tightly around, pressing and molding it with her fingers.

"Good." Dr. Emily straightened up from the table after a minute. "I think we're done. By the time Brock wakes up, he'll be able to walk on that leg just fine. We'd like to keep him in our wildlife unit overnight, just to make sure he has no side effects from the anesthetic."

Araminta Greenwood nodded. "I'll come pick him up in the morning."

As Mandy removed her white coat and hung it on the peg by the door, she couldn't help feeling worried. The badger was a wild animal, and she knew that too much interaction with humans was a bad idea. Would Ms. Greenwood really be looking after a wild animal for three whole weeks, until Brock's cast came off? She wondered how to ask without seeming rude.

Ms. Greenwood glanced at her. "I'll keep him fed and warm just until the cast comes off," she said, "but that's as far as I'll go. He's a wild animal, and I won't forget that." She smiled. "If that's what's worrying you."

Mandy blinked in surprise. "How did you know I was thinking that?"

Ms. Greenwood's eyes twinkled and she tapped the side of her nose.

Maybe she is a witch, after all, thought Mandy, feeling a shiver of fear and respect for the unusual woman.

In order to avoid crosscontamination with the domestic pets, the wild animals were kept in a separate residential unit. Mandy followed Simon and the sleeping badger over to the wildlife unit, where she filled an empty cage with clean straw. She was longing to pet the badger's rough, peppery fur, but she knew she wasn't supposed to touch the wild animals. Instead, she watched as Simon gently placed the badger into the cage.

"He'll wake up in half an hour or so," said Simon, shutting the cage door. "Then I bet he'll be hungry."

"What are you going to feed him?" Mandy asked as they washed their hands.

"Cat food," Simon said. He laughed at Mandy's expression. "Honestly! It's not as good as earthworms, but we aren't going to be digging up any of those for Brock tonight."

Ms. Greenwood was in the waiting room putting on her long black cape when Mandy returned. The cape smelled of moss and mushrooms and made Mandy wonder about the elderly woman's life in the middle of the woods.

Standing in the doorway of the second examining room, Dr. Adam was giving some instructions to Mrs. Ponsonby. Pandora's foot had a bandage on it, and Mrs. Ponsonby was cooing sympathetically and rubbing her face against the Peke's head.

"Come in and see us on Saturday, Mrs. Ponsonby,"

said Dr. Adam. "We'll check on that infection and change the dressing."

"Witch hazel," Araminta Greenwood suddenly remarked.

Mrs. Ponsonby turned pale and clutched Pandora tightly. "Don't you cast your spells on my little dog," she warned, sidling across the waiting room. "You and your witch . . . witch . . ."

"Hazel," Ms. Greenwood repeated, looking amused. "Good for taking care of infections. Only trying to help."

"Well, we don't need *that* sort of help," Mrs. Ponsonby said. She turned and walked extremely fast out of the waiting room, muttering something about magic under her breath.

"Don't mind Mrs. Ponsonby," Mandy said, worried that Ms. Greenwood was upset.

"Oh, I don't mind her," said Ms. Greenwood, picking up her hat and ramming it on her head. "Though it's clear that she does mind *me*. A lot. Until tomorrow, then." She marched out the door with her cape flowing behind her like water.

After a second, the door banged open again and James came running into the waiting room. "She's gone!" he said, panting.

"What are you talking about?" Mandy asked.

"That witch woman," said James. "She's gone already.

I was in the garden playing with Blackie, and I saw her come out of the clinic — and the next minute, I couldn't see her *anywhere*. Now look at me, and tell me she isn't a witch!" he concluded triumphantly.

Mandy put her hands in the air. "OK, she's a witch!" she said and laughed. After all, it *was* Halloween.

Four

"A *badger*?" James was amazed when Mandy told him about Ms. Greenwood and the contents of the box.

"He's beautiful," Mandy said enthusiastically. "Come and see." She dragged James off to the wildlife residential unit, where Simon was preparing the badger's lunch.

"Is Brock awake yet, Simon?" She peered into the cage, trying to see if the animal's eyes were open. The badger had his back to her, and it was impossible to tell.

"He'll be coming around shortly," Simon replied, mixing the cat food in a bowl. "If he doesn't wake up on his own, the smell of food should do it."

Because the badger was asleep, Mandy was able to

examine him more closely. She saw how the animal's fur darkened from its silvery tips to a deep browny-black close to the skin, and how his tiny ears were almost invisible, folded flat against his furry head.

The badger began to stir. He lifted his head and sniffed. At last, hampered by the bulky wrapping on its injured leg, he turned his large wedge-shaped body around in the straw and stared at them sleepily with a pair of dark, deep-set eyes.

"He's enormous," James murmured. "I didn't think they grew that big."

"Yes, this one's a record breaker all right," said Simon. He slipped the bowl of food through the bars of the cage and the badger began to eat right away.

"Mandy?" Dr. Emily poked her head around the unit door. "Your gran's on the phone. She wants to know something about this tail she's making for your Catwoman costume."

"Tail? Catwoman?" echoed Simon, raising his eyebrows.

Mandy grinned. "You'll have to come to our Halloween party to see," she said. "But only if you come in a costume."

"I'd better go," said James. "Mom's expecting me back for lunch."

"See you later, Brock," Mandy whispered to the badger when James had gone. "Don't worry, I promise it won't be long before you're back in the woods, eating yummy earthworms again."

The badger shook his broad head at her as if to say that cat food wasn't bad in the short term, and continued eating his food.

James came over first thing the next morning on his bike.

"Still worrying about Ms. Greenwood putting a spell on Blackie?" Mandy teased when she noticed that he hadn't brought the Labrador with him.

James didn't quite meet her eyes. "Just thought I'd come on my own today," he said. "It's really difficult keeping him on the leash when I'm on my bike." He quickly changed the subject. "Can we go and see the badger?"

Mandy's dad was just closing the door to the badger's cage when they came in. "Good news," he said with a smile. "Brock's doing well and showing no signs of stress or shock. I think we'll be handing him over to the capable hands of Ms. Greenwood this morning, as planned."

The badger started scratching his shaggy back on the wire mesh of his cage.

"Oh," Mandy said, feeling disappointed that the badger's stay at Animal Ark was over so soon. *Stop thinking like that*, she told herself firmly. *The badger needs to go back to the forest, and you know it.*

"I'm glad he's going home," said James sincerely. "It's wonderful to see him up close, but it doesn't feel right, seeing him in that cage. Do you know what I mean? He's just too . . . *wild*."

James was right. Mandy started to feel more cheerful at the thought of the badger snuffling through the leaves in the woods again, hunting for worms.

"He'll be in good hands while his leg gets better," said Dr. Adam. "Ms. Greenwood knows more about healing wild animals than any vet I know."

"I'm looking forward to seeing Ms. Greenwood again," Mandy said as her dad closed the door of the wildlife unit behind them.

"I'm not," said James.

Mandy rolled her eyes. "She's really nice, James. You'd like her if you just gave her a chance. She knows lots about animals."

"Hmm," James replied. "Snakes and newts and bats, too, I bet."

"All very topical, given the time of year," said Dr. Adam as they made their way back into the clinic. "How's your costume coming along, Mandy?"

"Gran called last night to tell me she's almost finished," Mandy said happily. "She's done something clever with a coat hanger inside my tail, so it curls up."

"An improvement on last year's squirrel, then," joked Mandy's dad, and Mandy punched him gently in the arm.

Ms. Greenwood was already waiting at the reception desk. She looked pleased when Dr. Adam gave her an update on how Brock was doing. "Half the battle with the wild ones is dealing with the shock," she said. "It can shut them down, stop them healing themselves. Sounds like he's made a good start."

"He shouldn't give you too much trouble," said Dr. Adam, handing her a bottle of painkillers and a set of feeding instructions. "Come back and see us in three weeks, when we can take that cast off."

Ms. Greenwood tucked the painkillers and the instructions somewhere deep in her black cape. Mandy noticed that her tights were striped yellow and green today. Then Simon emerged from the wildlife unit, carrying the badger in a traveling box. Mandy could just make out a pair of bright eyes looking through the small airholes in the side.

"I'll give you a hand loading him, Ms. Greenwood," said Simon. "Do you have some kind of vehicle?"

"A broomstick, probably," James whispered to Mandy.

"It's outside," Ms. Greenwood replied. "Follow me."

Mandy was a little disappointed not to see a neat,

twiggy broomstick leaning up against the wall outside the clinic. Instead, Ms. Greenwood marched up to a gleaming red mountain bike with a large basket attached to the handlebars.

James stepped forward, his mouth open. "Cool!"

"Glad you like it," said Ms. Greenwood while Simon strapped Brock's box firmly inside the basket. "Twenty-one gears, aluminum wheels, front and rear suspension." She gave James a wink. "Not exactly witchy, but very useful in the woods."

James blushed.

Ms. Greenwood tugged her hat on. "Got to run an errand or two in town, then we'll go home," she said. "Thanks for the help." She patted the box, making doubly sure that it was secure. Then she swung one yellow-and-green-striped leg over the saddle, pushed down on the pedals, and was out of sight within moments.

"No wonder Ms. Greenwood disappeared so quickly yesterday," Mandy remarked. "That bike looks really fast."

"OK, OK," James muttered. "But I still think she's a witch."

"I wish *I* were a witch," Mandy sighed as they walked around to the kitchen door. "I could do with some magic right now. I haven't even *started* the Halloween invitations, and the party's on Saturday. If we don't get them done today, no one will come."

"Don't worry," said James. "With two of us, it won't take long. Are we using those?" He pointed at the pile of black cards lying on the kitchen table.

Mandy nodded. "I thought we could use these, too," she said, and opened a plastic container that held two metallic gold pens, an orange gel pen, a tube of orange glitter and a small pot of glue.

"Great!" James said. "Come on, let's get started."

They settled down at the kitchen table and started planning the wording on the invitation. Then they wrote out several practice versions to see which one looked best.

Dr. Emily came into the kitchen for a quick cup of coffee. "Thank goodness you're starting those," she said, flicking on the kettle and scooping some instant coffee into her favorite mug. "I thought we might have to telephone everyone this year instead."

"It's all under control, Mom," Mandy assured her. "We're just deciding exactly what to write. Which of these sounds better? "Come and join the party in our spooky lair. Wear a groovy costume, spiders in your hair. That's the first one."

"That was mine," James put in proudly.

"And the second one is: 'Party fright and party shock, party starts at seven o'clock,'" Mandy read. "That's mine."

Dr. Emily took a sip of her coffee. "They're equally great," she said. "Why don't you use them both?"

They all looked around when the phone rang. Mandy was closest so she leaned over and picked up the receiver. It was John Hardy.

"You've got to come over!" he said as soon as Mandy had said hello.

Mandy blinked. "Right now?"

"Yes!" John insisted. "We've just gotten a package from Sara's sister in the States. They take Halloween really seriously there, and she's sent us some great American candy. I want you and James to come over and try it."

Mandy looked at the pile of black cards on the table. "We're supposed to be making the party invitations," she said.

"You can play with Brandy and Bertie, too," John said temptingly. "If you want."

That sealed it. *We can do the invitations later*, Mandy decided.

John didn't wait for Mandy's answer. "See you in fifteen minutes," he said, and put the phone down.

Mandy looked at James, who was staring expectantly at her. "John wants us to go and try these American candies his aunt sent him," she explained.

"Don't be too long," Dr. Emily warned. "The invitations won't make themselves."

"OK, Mom," Mandy said, grabbing her coat. "We'll see you later."

"And don't eat too much of that candy!" her mom called after her as she and James went into the yard to get their bikes. "You haven't had lunch yet!"

Mandy had to admit that it was much easier to ride without Blackie leaping around beside them. The road whizzed past beneath their wheels, and the sharp October air bit at their faces and made their noses red.

"Car!" James warned as they reached the crossroads outside the Fox and Goose. Mandy braked and brought her bike to the side of the road as a large green car drove past. Biscuit the golden retriever was looking out the back window. Mandy caught a glimpse of Matt Burness's face staring out beside the dog, and she raised her hand and waved. But Matt looked away, sullen and unresponsive.

John was waiting impatiently at the door of the Fox and Goose when Mandy and James dismounted. "I thought you'd never get here," he said.

"You only called us ten minutes ago!" Mandy protested.

John sighed. "Well, you're here now," he said. "Come in."

Mandy knew that John didn't mean to sound bossy. He just wasn't very good at chatting. *Sort of like Ms. Greenwood,* she decided.

They followed John around the back of the restaurant to the kitchen, where Sara Hardy was making a large pot of tomato and pepper soup for the lunchtime customers. The smell of warm rolls from the oven made Mandy's stomach rumble.

"Come to try the candy corn?" Sara asked.

Mandy was confused. "The candy what?"

"Candy corn," Sara smiled. "That's what this American candy is called. The box is over there, on the windowsill. Help yourself."

James peered inside the brightly colored box. "They look like little teeth!" he said, picking up a piece of candy corn and examining it.

"They're supposed to look like kernels of corn," John explained. "They're a great color for Halloween, aren't they?"

The candy corn was striped yellow, orange, and white. Mandy took a piece and bit into it. The sweet, fudgy taste was delicious. She closed her eyes, savoring the taste. "Perfect," she agreed. "Your parents can give

them out to trick-or-treaters. Once word gets around, the Fox and Goose will be really popular!"

"Do you want to take some for the party?" John offered.

"Thanks. We can fish them out of the powdered sugar instead of jelly beans," said James happily.

"Are you sure you can spare them?" Mandy asked.

"Oh, please take as many as you like," said Sara, wiping her hands on her apron. "The fewer there are in the house, the fewer I'll be tempted to eat."

"Do you want to come and see Brandy and Bertie?" said John. "I've put them in their run. Come on."

Mandy and James eagerly followed John out to the yard, where Walter Pickard's neighbor Ernie had made a large, roomy run with wire mesh stretched over a wooden frame. Weeds and lettuce leaves lay at one end, and a bowl of drinking water was at the other. Brandy and Bertie were running up and down, munching the leaves, and enjoying the pale October sunshine.

John's eyes shone as he scooped them both into his arms. "I'm sure they missed me," he said confidently. "Imogen looked after them really well, but it's not the same. Is it, guys?" He cuddled the two little rabbits under his chin. "Here, Mandy. You take Brandy," he said generously. "James, you can hold Bertie if you like."

They played with the rabbits, tickling their tummies and petting them while they talked about the party. When a bicycle-shaped shadow fell across the grass, Mandy looked up to see Ms. Greenwood pedaling past, the traveling box still strapped firmly into her basket.

"Ms. Greenwood must have finished her errand," she said, shading her eyes and watching the back of the woman's cape flapping in the wind like the wings of a giant crow. "I hope the badger's OK in that box."

"What badger?" John asked curiously.

Mandy and James told him about Brock while they put the rabbits back into their run.

"And you think she's a witch?" John asked with interest.

"*James* thinks she's a witch," Mandy corrected, laying her cheek on top of Brandy's soft brown head before putting him down next to the lettuce leaves. "I just think she knows a lot about herbs and animals and things like that."

"I bet she is a witch," John mused, shutting the mesh door of the run. He made his voice sound deep and spooky. "I bet she casts spells that make you go —"

"AAAAAHHH!"

A piercing scream echoed around the yard, and they all jumped out of their skins.

"That was Sara!" said John. He turned and ran back inside, with Mandy and James close behind.

In the kitchen, John's stepmother looked like she'd seen a ghost. Her face was white, and she was leaning against the kitchen table with one hand on her chest. "I've just had the scare of my life," she declared when they all rushed in. "Look at the candy corn! I swear it's moving!"

Mandy stared at the box on the windowsill. Sara was right. The candy was rustling and shivered as if it were alive. Then, like a small volcanic eruption, two black ears and a furry black head rose out of the orange-and-yellow candy. A pair of wide orange eyes blinked at them.

Mandy was so surprised she could barely speak. There was a *kitten* in the candy corn!

Five

The kitten tipped its head to one side and looked at its openmouthed audience. Several pieces of candy slid off its head and landed back in the box with a quiet *plop*.

"What on *earth* is a kitten doing in a box of candy?" Sara said at last.

The kitten shook its head and yawned, showing a pale pink mouth and a set of tiny sharp teeth.

"It's gorgeous," Mandy whispered.

"Do you think maybe it came all the way from the United States?" James asked in astonishment.

"The box was taped shut when it arrived," John told him. "A kitten wouldn't have survived the plane trip sealed in a box like that. It must have come through the window a couple of minutes ago." He pointed to the kitchen window, which was open slightly to let out the steam from Sara's soup.

"But the window's practically closed!" said James. "I know cats can squeeze through small spaces, but that's crazy!"

"Not as crazy as coming by mail," Mandy said. She walked slowly over to the box of candy without taking her eyes off the kitten. The little cat stared at her as she approached but didn't try to scramble out or burrow back into the candy corn. Mandy reached carefully into the box and tickled the kitten's head. The jet-black fur was warm and very soft. The kitten closed its eyes and let out a tiny rasping purr. Feeling encouraged, Mandy dug her other hand into the candy and gently lifted out the kitten.

"Now that's what I call a *black* cat," Sara remarked, coming closer to admire the little ball of fur that now sat cradled against Mandy's shoulder. "Look — not a speck of white on him! Or should I say her?"

Mandy looked at the kitten's tummy. "It's a boy," she said. Then she looked over the rest of the kitten, feeling for injuries the way her parents had shown her. There was a long scratch on his shoulder, which Mandy thought was probably a result of squeezing through the narrow window, and he was a little thin, but otherwise he seemed fine. Mandy guessed his age to be about six weeks, just old enough to leave his mother.

"So where did you come from, little fellow?" she asked, nuzzling him.

The kitten wriggled and gave the most extraordinary wailing meow that Mandy had ever heard. It wasn't so much a meow, she decided, as a yowl. Long and loud, it sounded like it should be coming from an animal twice the kitten's size.

"Whoa," said James, stepping back. "That's a spooky noise."

The hairs rose on the back of Mandy's neck as the kitten yowled his deep, mournful sound once again. "It's OK, little pussycat," she murmured. "You're safe with us."

"What's going on in here?" John's father, Julian Hardy, asked as he came into the kitchen. "First a scream, then a wail. Do we have ghosts?"

Mandy held out the kitten. "He just popped out of the candy corn! Isn't he sweet?"

"He's certainly a handsome little fellow," Mr. Hardy said with surprise. "But what's he doing here? He couldn't have come in the box of candy?"

Mandy felt the kitten tense. Before she could react, he sprang out of her arms and dug his tiny black claws into the sleeve of Mr. Hardy's sweater. Quick as a flash, he scrambled up Mr. Hardy's sleeve, ran across his shoulder, and came to rest on the top of his head.

"Wh-wh-," Mr. Hardy spluttered, waving his arms. The kitten clung on like a neat black wig, his ears pricked and his mouth slightly open as if he were laughing.

"Stay still!" Mandy grinned. "You'll frighten him."

"*I'll* frighten *him*?" Mr. Hardy echoed. "What about *me*? I'm not used to being treated as a pole to climb. And — ow! My head's not a pincushion! What are you doing up there?"

The kitten seemed to be enjoying the view and didn't want to come down.

"Take him into the restaurant like that, Dad," John begged, his eyes sparkling with laughter. "See if anyone notices."

Mr. Hardy obediently turned around and walked out of the kitchen. The kitten remained perfectly balanced on his head, crouched and steady. "Hey, does anyone recognize my hat?" Mandy heard Mr. Hardy ask. There was a burst of laughter and she peered through the door to watch what was going on.

It was nearly lunchtime, so the restaurant was almost full. Mr. Hardy stood with the kitten still clinging to his head. Ernie Bell was sitting at a table with a glass of juice in front of him and a broad grin on his face. "Suits you, Julian," he said.

"It's the fashion these days, Ernie," said Mr. Hardy with a grin. He looked upward. "You don't recognize this little fur ball, do you?"

"He's not yours?" Ernie said with surprise.

"Nope," said Mr. Hardy. "He just showed up in the kitchen. Can any of you help?"

Mandy saw people shaking their heads. No one seemed to know where the tiny black kitten had come from.

Suddenly, the kitten got bored. He took a flying leap

from the top of Mr. Hardy's head and landed in a blur of black fur on a table, where he raced up and down and batted at a couple of coasters. His paws shot out from beneath him as he skidded in a small puddle of water. With a look of great surprise on his face, he tried and failed to grip the table with his claws, slid gracefully along the polished wood, off the edge and straight into Ernie Bell's lap, where Ernie caught him like a ball.

"Well!" said Ernie as the laughter subsided, holding the small black cat up close to his face. "You're a feisty one, aren't you?"

The kitten curled up in Ernie's fingers and shut his eyes.

John's dad lifted the kitten out of Ernie's hands and brought him back into the kitchen. "No one out there could help, I'm afraid," he said sympathetically.

Mandy took the kitten from Mr. Hardy, and the huge orange eyes flew open. He yowled his peculiar yowl again as she cuddled him up against her sweatshirt. "It looks like we'll have to take you to Animal Ark," she said.

The kitten stretched and daintily pushed and pulled at Mandy's palms with his claws. Then he shot out of her hands and straight into the pouch at the front of her sweatshirt. Mandy felt him creep into the soft darkness, curl around on himself a couple of times, and settle down.

"You're even wearing your kitten-carrying outfit," Sara observed with a smile. "I'm sure your mom and dad will know what to do." She held out her hands apologetically. "I'm just sorry we can't help."

"Don't worry," said Mandy, putting one hand into her pouch and resting it on the kitten's back. He felt warm and cozy, his breathing quick and light. "We'll work something out."

"Let me hold him, Mandy," John begged. "Just for a minute."

Sara had given them all some soup for lunch since the kitten had seemed happy to stay in Mandy's pouch for a while. Then John insisted on coming back to Animal Ark with Mandy and James. Because of the kitten, Mandy was wheeling her bike with one hand while keeping the other one inside her pouch, petting her sleeping passenger. John was walking beside her, and James was riding as slowly as he could, wobbling precariously as he tried to keep pace with Mandy.

"He's still asleep," Mandy began. "Ouch!" She felt a sudden attack of tiny teeth on her thumb. She instinctively pulled her hand out of her pouch. The kitten came, too, his little body wrapped around her wrist and his teeth biting playfully at the fleshy part of her hand.

"Stop it, you little monkey!" Mandy protested, laugh-

ing. She stopped wheeling her bike and gently took hold
of the scruff of the kitten's neck to detach him from her
hand. He stopped biting at once and hung quietly from
her fingers, curled into a tight ball.

"Doesn't that hurt?" John asked anxiously.

"It's how his mother would carry him around," Mandy
explained, putting the kitten into John's outstretched
palms.

The kitten began to knead vigorously at John's hands,
first with one paw and then with the other. John flinched,
laughing.

The three friends made their way slowly to Animal
Ark, taking turns carrying the kitten. The little black cat
was endlessly entertaining. One minute he was completely still, and the next he was scrambling up a sleeve
or burrowing under a sweater. It was almost as if he had
a tiny switch of energy that flicked on and off in an instant.

At last they walked into the Animal Ark kitchen,
where Mandy's parents were clearing away their lunch.

"Wait till you see what we have," Mandy said breath-
lessly.

Mandy's dad looked wary. "A tarantula?" he asked.

Mandy rolled her eyes. "Where am I going to get a
tarantula in Welford?"

"I never know what you're going to produce next, Mandy," her dad replied. "Come on. Show us."

Mandy put her hand carefully into her pocket and took out the kitten. Exhausted from playing most of the way from the Fox and Goose, he had fallen asleep again and didn't move.

"What a darling!" Mandy's mother exclaimed. "Where did you find it?"

"Him," Mandy corrected. "I checked."

"He popped out of a box of candy," John informed them.

Dr. Adam started to say something, then raised his hands. "I won't ask," he said with a grin. "Whose is he?"

"We don't know," Mandy confessed. She quickly explained what had happened at the Fox and Goose.

"We'd better put up a sign in the clinic," said Dr. Emily. "We can see if anyone comes forward when they realize he's missing."

"But did he escape from somewhere, is he lost, or was he abandoned?" Dr. Adam wanted to know. "If it's one of the first two, then maybe there's a chance someone will claim him. But if it's the third . . ."

He didn't need to finish the sentence. With a heavy heart, Mandy knew what he meant. If the kitten had been abandoned, no one was going to claim him and take him back to a loving home. She bent her head and kissed the sleeping kitten between the ears. *How could anyone lose you?* she thought wistfully. *If you were mine, I wouldn't let you out of my sight.*

"May he stay in the residential unit tonight?" she asked.

"Of course," her dad replied. "But you know the rules, Mandy. Tonight, and *only* tonight."

Mandy did know the rules. It was impossible to keep every lost or abandoned animal that came to Animal Ark. It was a rule that seemed really hard at times, but she understood why her parents insisted on keeping it.

The kitten woke up. He opened his eyes very wide at the sight of so many faces peering down at him and started purring loudly.

"He obviously likes people," Dr. Adam said. "That's a good sign."

The kitten gave one of his long, loud yowls.

"That sounds Burmese," Dr. Emily said with surprise, scooping up the kitten and looking closely at him. "The color's wrong, but I bet there's Burmese ancestry somewhere. What do you think, Adam?"

The kitten blinked his wide, jewellike eyes and yowled again.

"He sounds more like a police siren than a Burmese cat," Dr. Adam remarked, looking over his wife's shoulder. "But that would fit with his friendly nature. Burmese cats are very much like dogs in that way — they love to be around people. I haven't seen a Burmese with orange eyes before, though."

"Actually, they can have eyes that color," John said unexpectedly. "I've read about them. They can have any color from green to orange."

The kitten yowled again and struggled.

"He must be hungry," Mandy said. "Can we feed him some of Brock's cat food?"

"He's still very young," said her mom. "I think he'll just need milk for now. Then we'll see if he's still hungry and judge whether or not he needs some solid food as well."

She put the kitten on the floor, where he immediately started chasing his tiny tail. When Mandy set the bowl of warmed milk down beside him, the kitten lapped at it with great concentration, milky droplets trembling on his threadlike whiskers. Then he stopped drinking and gave a huge yawn.

"Up you come," said Mandy, picking up the sleepy kitten and setting him down on a cushion that James had brought from the living room and put on the kitchen table. The kitten curled up with his nose tucked under his tail.

"I could stay here and watch that kitten all day," said

Dr. Emily, smiling. "But we've got work to do. You'll get back to making those invitations now, won't you?"

Mandy had forgotten all about the party invitations since finding the kitten. "Of course," she promised. "There are three of us now, so it won't take long."

John was happy to stay and help and came up with the great idea of carving some potatoes into spooky shapes and using them as stamps. When Mandy asked what they could use for paint, John showed her how to unscrew the end of one of the gold metallic pens and tip out the ink onto a paper plate. Soon they were stamping their black cards with golden ghosts and spiders, trying not to drip the glittering ink on the wooden tabletop.

Mandy was so absorbed in making the invitations that she didn't notice the kitten wake up with a brisk shake of his head and a yawn.

"Uh-oh," said James. "Mandy, you'd better catch him before" — the little black cat jumped down from the cushion and stepped daintily into the paper plate containing the golden ink — "he steps in the ink," James finished.

Mandy reached out to grab the kitten, but she wasn't quick enough. He sprang into the air and landed in a puddle of gold, right in the middle of the table. Then he ran full tilt across the scattered invitations, leaving a trail of tiny golden footprints behind him before bunching up and leaping at the gingham curtains that framed the kitchen window.

"Oh, no!" Mandy said, gasping as she stood up. "Mom's curtains!"

Splidge, splodge — more gold footprints followed the kitten up the curtain and along the top of the curtain rod. Mandy tried to catch the kitten, but he was too quick. He leaped nimbly down from the curtain rod, shot into a saucepan, and then hurtled out again, coming to rest inside the carved pumpkin Mandy had placed on the windowsill a few days earlier. Luckily, there was no candle inside it.

Mandy didn't know whether to laugh or cry. She peered inside the carved pumpkin and saw the kitten staring up at her with his perfect pumpkin-colored eyes.

She turned around and grinned at James and John. "Well, that's one problem solved at least," she said. "I think we should call him Pumpkin. Can you imagine a better name for a Halloween kitten?"

Six

James propped the invitations up on the windowsill so the ink could dry, while Mandy and John cleaned up after Pumpkin as best they could. The gold ink came off the tabletop easily enough, but the curtains were a different matter.

"I'll have to take them down and wash them," Mandy said glumly. "Mom'll be angry otherwise." She glanced at Pumpkin, who was sitting on his cushion and licking himself clean. "You are *trouble*," she said, wagging her finger at the kitten.

Pumpkin yowled, his pale pink tongue glittering faintly with the gold ink he was removing from his paws.

"What are you going to do with him?" John asked.

Mandy sighed. "I'd love to keep him, but Mom and Dad won't let me. So I guess we need to make some posters to put up around town and on the clinic bulletin board."

"Hello! Anyone in?" Mandy's gran came through the kitchen door, carrying an armful of fake fur. "Hello, Mandy, dear," she said, putting the pile of black cloth down on the table. "Here's your costume — oh!" She spotted Pumpkin, who was fast asleep on the cushion. "What a lovely little thing! Where did you find him?"

Mandy explained. Grandma Hope listened and petted the kitten lightly on the head with one finger. Pumpkin didn't move.

"What a shame," she said when Mandy had finished. "Still, I'm sure you'll find his owner soon. Are you using this black paper to make posters?"

"Actually, we've been using that for the party invitations," Mandy said.

"Well, when you finish those, perhaps you can use the rest to make some posters," Gran suggested.

Mandy looked thoughtfully at the pens, glitter, card, and ink scattered over the kitchen table. "We *could* use up the rest of this stuff," she said. "After all, with his black fur and orange eyes, he's a Halloween cat, isn't he?"

"I'll make a potato cutout of a cat, if you like," John offered.

"And we can use the orange glitter for his eyes," added James.

Mandy smiled gratefully. "That would be fantastic," she said. "We can distribute the posters when we deliver the party invitations."

"I'm sure someone will want him," Gran said reassuringly. "He's such a sweet kitten that even if he has been abandoned, you shouldn't have any trouble finding a new home for him."

"I hope not," Mandy said.

"Now then." Gran picked up a long piece of black fur from the pile she had put on the table. "I just need to adjust the fastening for your tail, Mandy. Arms up, like a good girl."

Mandy obediently lifted her arms while her grandmother looped a tape measure around her middle. After a swift adjustment, she put the tail belt around Mandy's waist and fastened it.

"I love it!" Mandy exclaimed, looking over her shoulder at her new black tail. It fit perfectly, curling up at the end just like a real cat's.

"How did you know, Mrs. Hope?" John asked curiously.

Mandy's grandmother turned to look at him, puzzled. "Know what, dear?"

"About Pumpkin," John said. He sounded baffled.

"We just found him today. How did you make Mandy a costume so quickly?"

"I wasn't planning to look like Pumpkin," Mandy said with a grin. "I was going to be Catwoman. But you've given me a great idea, John." She twirled around, and her tail flew out behind her. "From now on, I'm going to be Pumpkin instead!"

The sky was dark and forbidding the following day. Although it wasn't raining, it was the sort of weather where rain looked like it was just around the next corner. Mandy cycled into town with posters inside her sweatshirt, which she had tucked into her jeans to stop the posters from slithering out. James was waiting for her at the post office, ready to take the invitations and posters around to their friends. He had Blackie with him today because they would be cycling slowly with all the posters and invitations to deliver.

Blackie was delighted to see Mandy and wriggled around her legs as she dismounted and leaned her bicycle up against the post office wall.

"No Pumpkin?" James asked.

Mandy reached down and rubbed Blackie behind his shoulders, making him squirm with pleasure. "Pumpkin's keeping Mom and Dad busy today for a change," she said.

James grinned. "I'm glad you weren't late," he said, rubbing his hands together and shivering. "I hate dark days like this. It feels like the middle of the night, and it's only lunchtime. Do you think it'll take long to pass out the posters?"

"I hope not," Mandy said, taking out the first one and smoothing the wrinkles out of it. "I don't want to be out in this weather for long, either."

James tied Blackie up outside the shop. They pushed open the post office door, glad to be out of the cold, and looked around. Mr. McFarlane, who ran the post office, was nowhere to be seen.

"Hello!" Mandy called. "Is anyone here? Mr. McFarlane?"

Mrs. McFarlane appeared at the back of the shop. She was looking uncharacteristically solemn. "You'll find my husband outside," she said. "He's not in the best of moods today. May I help?"

"We were just wondering," Mandy began. Then she paused. "Why is Mr. McFarlane in a bad mood?" she asked cautiously.

Mrs. McFarlane pursed her lips. "Vandals," she said. "They paid us a visit in the night. Scrawled all kinds of rubbish on the wall that my poor husband is having to clean up. Honestly!" She said. "As if we didn't have enough to do."

Mandy thought back to the conversation she'd had with Mrs. Ponsonby and Mrs. Parker Smythe the day that Ms. Greenwood had arrived with the injured badger. First there was the broken flowerpot at the Fox and Goose, and now this. She had an odd, sick sensation in the pit of her stomach, imagining how she'd feel if someone did this at Animal Ark.

The post office door tinkled and Mr. McFarlane came in, looking tired and annoyed. He was holding a bucket of soapy water and a scrub brush, and his shirtfront was wet and dirty. "Please put the kettle on, dear," he said wearily to his wife. "I need a strong cup of tea."

He noticed Mandy and James. "What do you two want?" he asked.

"We're very sorry about the graffiti, Mr. McFarlane," James said.

Mr. McFarlane grunted. "So am I," he said. "I don't suppose you know anything about it, do you?"

Mandy shook her head, hoping her expression wasn't giving anything away. Was it really possible that Matt Burness had something to do with this? The handsome face of Biscuit the golden retriever kept looming in her mind.

"What may I do for you, anyway?" asked Mr. McFarlane, setting down his bucket and brush.

Mandy held out a poster. "We were wondering if we

could put this up on your bulletin board," she said politely. "If it's not too much trouble." She explained about Pumpkin as quickly as she could, while Mr. McFarlane looked at the poster.

"FOUND!" the poster read, its printed gold letters standing out clearly against the black paper. "One black kitten, in need of a good home." Halfway down the poster was a gold potato-stamp of a kitten, with two specks of orange glitter for eyes, followed by Animal Ark's phone number.

"I have more things to worry about than a homeless kitten," Mr. McFarlane grumbled, but he took the poster anyway. "And if you see any brutes hanging around, give them a piece of my mind for me, won't you?" he called after them as they left the shop.

"Poor Mr. McFarlane," said Mandy as they walked toward the Fox and Goose to pick up John.

"I told you Matt Burness was trouble," said James.

"But his dog . . ." Mandy began.

"It's not his *dog* who's been painting walls," James reminded her. "Just because he has a nice dog doesn't mean he's a nice person, Mandy."

Mandy thought about this when they reached the Fox and Goose. She knew James was right, but she felt miserable just the same.

John was waiting for them, stamping his feet in the

cold. "Dad said he'd put a few posters up in the restaurant," he said, walking out to meet Mandy and James on the road. "I know nobody could help last time he asked, but different people come into the place all the time. You never know."

"True," Mandy said, nodding. "Jean let me put two on the bulletin board at Animal Ark. Mom said she'd put up a couple in the town hall at her next yoga class, too. At this rate, we'll get rid of them all really fast!"

They dropped in on Mandy's grandparents at Lilac Cottage first. "We'll take two posters," Mandy's grandpa declared. "One for the front window, and one for the window of the camper. How's that?"

"Thanks, Grandpa," Mandy said. She picked up Smoky, her grandparents' cat, and cuddled him. "Oh, and here's your invitation for Saturday night, too, before I forget."

Mandy's grandmother adjusted her glasses so she could read the invitation out loud. "'Come and join the party in our spooky lair. Wear a groovy costume, spiders in your hair,'" she read. "That sounds marvelous, Mandy. I can't promise any spiders, but we'll dress up a little!"

"We only have two posters left," said James as they walked down the main street toward the church. "Let's put one on the parish bulletin board. Then everyone who comes through town will see it."

Suddenly, Mandy stopped walking. In the park, she could see a group of four boys hanging around the pond.

"Uh-oh," said James, stopping beside her.

Blackie gave a strange growl in the back of his throat as Mandy stepped forward to get a better look at the boys. It was hard to tell in the dull afternoon light, but one of them looked like he was wearing a green base-ball cap.

"I think that's Matt Burness," she said, her heart sinking.

James sighed. "Doesn't surprise me," he replied, tuck-ing his chin into the collar of his coat. "Come on, let's go the other way."

There was a splash, followed by a shout. One of the boys had thrown an empty soda can into the pond. The ducks in the middle of the water squawked in alarm, flapping their wings and taking cover on the far side.

"The poor ducks!" Mandy said indignantly. "I'm going to say something."

James caught her arm. "Don't," he pleaded, dragging her back. "I have to see them at school next week. I don't want any trouble."

"They aren't worth bothering with, Mandy," said John. He sounded disgusted. "Let's just do what James says."

Mandy reluctantly followed James and John, looking

back over her shoulder. Matt was talking and laughing with the others and kicking another can along the side of the pond.

They walked on until they reached the woods at the edge of town.

"One more poster to go," said John. "What should we do with it?"

"I thought we could give it to Mrs. Ponsonby," Mandy said. "She invites lots of people to Bleakfell Hall for coffee and things. Come on, we can take the path through the woods."

James looked slightly pale. "Do we have to?"

"What are you worried about, James?" Mandy asked mischievously. "Mrs. Ponsonby or the woods?"

"I'm not worried," James said unconvincingly. "Blackie is."

It was true that Blackie kept close to James as they picked their way along the narrow path under the trees. Dark branches loomed over their heads, cutting off what was left of the dwindling daylight, while shadows stretched down around them, filled with secretive rustlings and the occasional *chack* of a bird.

"Ms. Greenwood lives in these woods somewhere," Mandy said. "I wonder how Brock is?"

James stopped dead. "I wish you hadn't reminded me of that, Mandy," he said nervously.

John's eyes gleamed in the fading daylight. "Where's her house?"

Mandy shrugged. "I don't know exactly."

"She could be watching us now," John whispered. "Dusk is the perfect time for witches."

"Don't talk like that," James said with a shiver. Blackie whined and pressed himself closer to James's legs.

"It's best to be prepared," John went on melodramatically. "Maybe Ms. Greenwood's house scuttles around on little legs so she can follow her victims through the woods and boil her witchy brews at the same time!"

"Don't be silly," Mandy said. Even she was starting to feel scared. "Come on. Bleakfell Hall's just another five minutes farther."

They continued walking, in silence this time. The darkness seemed to press down on them like a thick blanket, and twigs snapped extra loudly under their feet. Mandy was beginning to wish that John would start talking again, when an owl suddenly hooted somewhere above them.

WHO-HOO . . .

Blackie yelped in terror and bolted off the path, his leash tangling around James's legs. James fell over with a crunch and a yell of pain, skidding off the path and into the wet carpet of leaves that littered the forest floor.

Mandy ran over to where he was lying. "Are you OK?" she asked urgently.

James blinked behind his glasses, which were skewed on his nose. "My . . . ankle," he said through gritted teeth.

Blackie came slinking back, his leash trailing through the leaves and his tail tucked between his legs. He started licking James's face apologetically.

"Don't worry, Blackie." Mandy patted the Labrador. "It wasn't your fault."

James heaved himself on his elbows and tried to get up. But he fell back again with another grunt of pain.

"Can you walk?" Mandy asked, concerned.

James shook his head. "Don't think so."

Mandy looked around. The woods was now looking really dark, and she began to feel frightened. James was too heavy to carry back, but they couldn't leave him here. What were they going to do?

Swish. Swish. Swish.

John swung around. "What was that?"

"Just leaves," Mandy said, an icy feeling creeping up her neck.

"You mean, someone walking *through* leaves," James whispered, his eyes round and fearful.

Swish. Swish. The whispery sound was growing louder. Someone was coming. Mandy felt a moment of blind terror as she stared into the trees. It was all she could do not to scream out loud when a tall, dark figure stepped onto the path.

"Dear, dear," said Araminta Greenwood. "Whatever's happened here?"

Seven

Mandy felt faint with relief. "Ms. Greenwood!" she exclaimed. "We were just talking about you!"

Araminta Greenwood's face was unreadable in the darkness. "Yes, I imagine you were," she said drily. She swept her black cape out of the way and knelt down beside James. "What happened to you, young man?" she asked.

James smiled a little nervously. "I hurt my ankle," he said, pointing at his right foot.

Ms. Greenwood felt James's anklebone with firm but gentle fingers. "Hmm," she said, standing up. "No broken bones this time. Nasty sprain, though. Come on. We'll fix you up back at the house."

She suddenly noticed John, who was hanging back in the shadows. "And who are you?" she inquired.

Mandy made the introductions as John stared hard at his feet.

"Pleased to meet you," said Ms. Greenwood, smiling unexpectedly. "You all look frozen half to death. Hot chocolate at the house. Come on."

She lifted James up as if he were a feather, turned her back, and vanished.

"Where did she go?" John asked.

Blackie flung back his head and howled. Ms. Greenwood had been there one minute and was gone the next. It was uncanny.

Mandy grabbed Blackie's leash and ran in what she hoped was the right direction. "Ms. Greenwood?" she called. "Where are you?"

There was a glimmer of yellow-and-red-striped tights as Ms. Greenwood turned around. With her back to Mandy and John, her long black cape had been the perfect camouflage in the dark woods. "The house is right up here," she called. "Follow the light!"

Mandy noticed a faint, ghostly flickering in the trees. It looked like candlelight. She almost laughed out loud, picturing James's face if they'd seen the flickering in the middle of John's spooky storytelling.

"I really thought Ms. Greenwood had vanished just then," John said, panting and appearing beside Mandy.

"Serves you right for telling scary stories," Mandy scolded, with a grin to show she didn't mean it.

They waded on through the damp brown leaves, following an invisible path between the trees until they reached a clearing. In the middle of the clearing sat a neat stone house with a row of carved pumpkins glowing in the windows. Blackie sniffed with interest at the woven willow fence and hazelwood gate that separated the yard of the house from the forest.

Mandy pushed open the gate and stared around at the carefully planted rows of vegetables in the garden and the clumps of fragrant herbs that lined the mossy path. Light flowed like honey through the cracks around Ms. Greenwood's front door, and wood smoke spiraled out of the chimney.

"It's like the gingerbread house in 'Hansel and Gretel,'" said John in a low voice.

"But Ms. Greenwood isn't going to eat us," Mandy pointed out.

"How do *you* know?" John replied darkly.

Ignoring him, Mandy tied Blackie to a heavy boot

scraper that sat on the doorstep, and she pushed open the door.

The house seemed to consist of one large room lit by dozens of candles and a blazing log fire. Herbs and flowers hung drying from the rafters, and misshapen bottles containing leaves and powders lined the long shelves above an old black stove. A tray of warm cookies sat cooling on a wire rack next to it. Ms. Greenwood was stoking the fire, and the flames leaped merrily upward. Mandy couldn't help thinking that it was the perfect witch's house. There was even a pot that looked like a small cauldron hanging on a hook over the fireplace.

John stopped dead on the doorstep and looked wide-eyed at the cauldron.

"Don't be scared," said Ms. Greenwood. She looked smaller and less forbidding without her cape. "Come in and have a cookie."

John sidled in and sat down next to James, who was lying on a long, low sofa. He looked uncertainly at the cookies.

Ms. Greenwood gave a brisk, barking laugh. "They won't poison you," she said. "Mandy? How about you?"

The cookie was warm and chewy, with an odd taste that Mandy couldn't quite identify. "Delicious," she said gratefully. "What's in it?"

"Spiced nettle," Ms. Greenwood said. "My own recipe."

John cautiously helped himself to a cookie. He took a tiny nibble, and then another. Before long, the cookie had disappeared.

Ms. Greenwood straightened up from the fire. "Mandy," she said, "I'm going to need some comfrey for James's ankle. It's growing underneath the window. Could you pick some for me?"

She swung the cauldronlike pot over the fire on its cleverly rotating hook and poured in several ladles of water from a small barrel beside the log pile.

"What does comfrey look like?" Mandy asked.

"Sturdy little thing with gray-green, spearlike leaves. You can't miss it."

After hunting around, Mandy found the comfrey growing in a sheltered corner under the window. She carefully picked a handful of the thick, slightly furry leaves and went back inside, where the warm smell of cookies had been replaced by the distinctive smell of boiling cabbage. Mandy couldn't help wrinkling her nose as she gave Ms. Greenwood the leaves.

"Cabbage and comfrey," Ms. Greenwood explained, noticing Mandy's expression. She stirred the leaves into the pot. "It'll help to bring down the swelling. Country folk don't call comfrey 'knitbone' for nothing."

When the mixture was ready, Ms. Greenwood ladled

the steaming comfrey and cabbage poultice onto a clean woolen cloth and placed it gently on James's ankle.

"That's amazing," James said after a minute. "It feels better already." He wiggled his toes experimentally and winced.

"It won't heal all at once," Ms. Greenwood warned. "But it's a good start."

There was a strange shuffling sound in the corner of the room, and a squat furry figure waddled into view.

"Brock!" Mandy exclaimed in delight. "I didn't know you were there."

The badger sniffed the air with a funny, nodding motion and shuffled around a little more. John, who hadn't seen a badger close up before, was almost speechless with amazement, and Mandy noticed that he lifted his feet off the floor as if Brock might nibble at his toes.

"How is Brock doing, Ms. Greenwood?" asked James.

"Very well." Ms. Greenwood poured out four cups of hot chocolate. "He got used to the cast very quickly. He's out most of the time, hunting as best he can in the garden, but he likes to come in now and then."

"Does he sleep here?" John asked, his eyes fixed wonderingly on the wild animal.

"On and off," Ms. Greenwood replied. She handed out the hot chocolate. Mandy took hers gratefully and cupped it between her hands. The heat spread through her fingers and up her arms, warming her all over.

Araminta Greenwood settled herself comfortably in a shabby green armchair beside the fire and regarded her visitors. "So," she said, "had you planned this visit, or did our paths simply cross by chance?"

"We were on our way to give this to Mrs. Ponsonby," Mandy said. She pulled the remaining poster from beneath her sweatshirt, straightened it out, and showed it to Ms. Greenwood, who read it thoughtfully.

"Kitten, eh?" she remarked. "Never liked cats myself. I've always found them to be rather selfish creatures."

"That depends on the cat!" Mandy protested. "There are as many different kinds of cats as there are people. Like Burmese or Siamese cats — they are really friendly and sociable, more like dogs in some ways. I'm sure you could find a cat to suit you, Ms. Greenwood."

"Hmm." Ms. Greenwood sounded unconvinced. "How do you happen to have this kitten, anyway?"

"It's a really sad story," Mandy began.

Craaaa! A horrible, hoarse screech filled the room from somewhere up in the chimney. Mandy jumped to her feet, her hands over her ears. James almost fell off the sofa, while John gave a yell and spilled half his hot chocolate on his sweater.

"Wh-what was that?" Mandy stammered.

"That's just Cor," Ms. Greenwood said calmly, refilling her mug from the pot. "He's no nightingale, but he doesn't mean any harm."

"Who is Cor?" James asked.

Ms. Greenwood smiled. "He's a crow. Cor's short for his Latin name, *Corvus*. He fell out of his nest and broke his wing as a youngster, and I rescued him." She nodded out the window. "He's never really gotten the hang of flying and lives outside in a hutch. He's a noisy old thing, but we get along just fine."

Another jarring screech floated down the chimney.

"That must be what Mrs. Ponsonby heard," Mandy said. "That time when she was walking her dogs in the woods. No wonder she thinks you're a witch, Ms. Greenwood!" She clapped her hand to her mouth in dismay, wondering if she'd sounded very rude.

Ms. Greenwood reached for a nettle cookie. "I know my reputation," she said matter-of-factly. "Tell you the truth, it suits me. Never cared much for company. Folks leave me alone, and I like it that way."

It was really dark now, and Mandy could barely see the trees outside. Her mom and dad would be worried. "Excuse me, Ms. Greenwood," she said, "but may I use your phone? It's getting late, and I should call my parents."

"Haven't got a telephone, I'm afraid," Ms. Greenwood apologized. "Never needed one."

Mandy's face fell. How were they going to get home? They didn't have their bikes, and James couldn't walk.

Ms. Greenwood saw her concern. "Why don't you borrow my bicycle and go get your parents?" she suggested. "There's a helmet and some lights by the door. The bicycle is outside, by the gate."

"OK," said Mandy, making up her mind. "It'll take me about ten minutes to ride to Animal Ark. I'll get Mom or Dad to come here in the Land Rover."

John looked nervous at the prospect of being left behind with Ms. Greenwood. James didn't look very happy, either. Mandy smiled encouragingly at them. "I won't be long," she promised.

Outside, she glanced hopefully around the garden for Cor, but the crow was nowhere to be seen. Ms. Greenwood fitted the lights to the bike and showed Mandy how the brakes worked. Then she handed her a helmet.

"Go carefully now," she advised. "The path is rough. And don't worry about your friends. We'll be fine until you get back." Her eyes twinkled. "Though it's clear that they expect me to eat them as soon as you've gone!"

Mandy was out of the woods within five minutes, feeling very relieved at how easily Ms. Greenwood's bike negotiated the ruts and puddles on the muddy path. It wasn't long before she was pedaling into town. Steering the bike carefully, she swung around the corner by the park and almost ran straight into Matt Burness, who was standing by the side of the road.

Mandy swerved and put her leg down to stop herself from falling off the bike.

Matt Burness stepped forward. "Are you OK?" he said, sounding concerned.

Matt's friends appeared behind him. "Who's this, Matt?" The tallest of the three boys looked Mandy up and down. His dark, deep-set eyes were unfriendly. "Your girlfriend?"

Matt stepped back from Mandy as if he'd been stung.

"I know that bike!" exclaimed one of the others, a stocky blond boy with a pimple on his chin. "That crazy witch was riding it yesterday!"

The tall boy's eyes narrowed. "It belongs to the witch?"

Mandy glared at him. "She's not a witch," she said.

"She's not a witch," the boy mocked, imitating Mandy's voice. His friends laughed. Matt laughed, too, but quietly, as if he felt uncomfortable. "You must be a friend of hers if you're defending her," the tall boy continued. "We don't like the witch." He leaned forward and thrust his face aggressively toward Mandy. "She's someone who should keep her opinions to herself."

It sounded as if Ms. Greenwood had told the boys off the day before. Mandy felt glad.

"We don't like the witch," the boy continued, "so I guess we don't like *you*." He grabbed one of the gleaming red handlebars of the bike. "Nice bike, though," he added slyly.

"Get out of my way," Mandy snapped. She tried to push past the boys, but they laughed and grabbed at the handlebars. Matt joined in, but Mandy noticed that he avoided her eyes.

Suddenly, two bright headlights swung around the corner. The boys blinked and shielded their eyes. The tall ringleader leaned toward Mandy and hissed, "We know where that witch lives, you know. Tell her to expect a visit from us sometime soon!"

Then they all melted into the darkness as Dr. Adam's Land Rover noisily, wonderfully, rolled up beside Mandy.

Eight

"Dad!" Mandy exclaimed. She'd never been so happy to see anyone in her life.

Dr. Adam opened the Land Rover door and stepped into the road. "Where on earth have you been, Mandy?" he asked. Then he frowned. "And who were those boys?"

"I'll tell you later," Mandy replied. "Come on. We've got to go to Ms. Greenwood's. James has hurt his ankle."

She told her dad the whole story while he loaded the bike into the back of the Land Rover. "Ms. Greenwood's house is incredible," she confided, climbing into the passenger seat. "She even has a pet crow living there!"

"Ms. Greenwood is a law unto herself," her dad agreed.

Just then the glove compartment gave a familiar, yowling meow.

"Is that Pumpkin?" Mandy asked with surprise. She bent down to peer into the open glove compartment and was amazed to see the little kitten curled up on a pair of thick woolen gloves.

"Ah," said her dad, shifting gears as he swung off the road and onto the muddy forest track. "My stowaway has woken up. I was on my way to High Point Farm when he popped up on the backseat. He gave me the scare of my life! He disappeared earlier, and we spent ages trying to find him." He looked down at the kitten, who was stumbling around in Mandy's hands and making her laugh. "It was too late to take him home, so I put him in the glove compartment."

Mandy saw the glimmer of a chocolate bar wrapper lurking under the gloves. "And that's not all you put in the glove compartment!" she exclaimed. "Chocolate, Dad? What about your diet?"

"I need extra energy on cold evening calls," her dad protested. "Don't tell Mom, will you?"

They drove up to Ms. Greenwood's house, and Dr. Adam turned off the engine. The sudden quiet made Pumpkin yowl, so Mandy tucked him quickly into her sweatshirt pouch. She felt the kitten curl around and around several times before settling down for another snooze.

Soon they were all inside, eating Ms. Greenwood's nettle cookies while Mandy told everyone about the boys in town.

"It's disgraceful!" Dr. Adam exclaimed. "Who are their parents? I've a good mind to have a word with them."

"The ringleader sounds like Adam Poole," said James, frowning. "The blond one you described is his sidekick, Ben Stevens. And I'd guess the third one is Liam Collins. They always hang around with Matt at school, making trouble."

"They recognized your bike, Ms. Greenwood," Mandy said, turning to her. "Did you speak to them yesterday?"

"I certainly did," Ms. Greenwood replied. "The wretches were throwing cans at the ducks on the pond. I told them what I thought of their behavior."

"I don't like the sound of that threat they made about paying you a visit," Dr. Adam said.

Ms. Greenwood gave a dismissive snort. "They don't scare me."

Mandy's dad checked his watch. "We should take James and that ankle to see Dr. Mason tonight. We'll catch him if we hurry." He looked around the room.

"And on the subject of injured legs, how is Brock the badger?"

As if in answer to his question, two bright eyes and a striped snout appeared around the side of Ms. Greenwood's armchair. Mandy felt the same thrill of excitement that she'd had two days earlier when Brock had come to the clinic. *I'll never get tired of looking at him,* she thought.

"He's getting better," Ms. Greenwood replied. She stood up and moved to the other side of the fire so the badger wouldn't feel too crowded. He shuffled out from behind the armchair and blinked shortsightedly at them all before heading for a bowl of cat food beside the front door.

Mandy felt a twitch in her sweatshirt pocket. Pumpkin had woken up. "Ms. Greenwood?" she said hesitantly, remembering what Araminta had said about not liking cats. "Do you remember the kitten on our poster?"

"Of course," Ms. Greenwood replied, looking surprised at the question.

Mandy pulled Pumpkin gently from her pocket. Surely Ms. Greenwood would change her mind about cats when she saw how cute the kitten was. "Well," she said, "here he is."

She held Pumpkin out for Ms. Greenwood to admire, but the woman made no move to pet the kitten's soft black fur. "Very nice," she said briskly, "if you like cats."

A little crestfallen, Mandy started to put Pumpkin back in her pocket. But the kitten was in the mood for adventure. He took a flying leap from Mandy's hands and landed in the middle of Ms. Greenwood's rug, where he energetically attacked a loose thread with his claws.

"Don't let him anywhere near Brock," Ms. Greenwood warned. "A kitten would make a fine supper for a hungry badger."

As if in slow motion, Mandy saw the badger shuffling back to his place behind the armchair. Pumpkin looked at the passing badger with interest and pounced on his tail.

Brock whipped around, his jaws wide open. The kitten jumped sideways just in time, his stubby tail bristling with terror. John tried to grab him as he whisked by, but he was off across the sofa and up the curtains in a flash. He flew from the curtain rod to the fringed lampshade that hung from the ceiling, dug his claws tightly into the faded silk shade, and yowled with fear and misery.

"Oh!" Mandy cried in dismay. She reached for

Pumpkin, but the lampshade was just out of reach. Seeing the kitten swinging there with terror in his eyes
made Mandy feel awful. *He's still so young*, she thought
unhappily. *He should be with his mother.* What was she
going to do if no one claimed him? The little cat needed
a good home — not just a pocket in Mandy's sweatshirt
or a cage at the Welford Cat Rescue Center.

Ms. Greenwood calmly reached up and plucked the
coal-black kitten from the lampshade as if she were
picking an apple from a tree. "That was close, little cat,"
she said, petting the trembling kitten with one finger.
"Perhaps that will teach you a few manners. Badgers
don't like to be toyed with."

Pumpkin yowled pathetically and tried to burrow
into Ms. Greenwood's large, furry sweater. Against the
black wool, the only part of the kitten that was visible
were his blazing orange eyes.

"That's quite a noise," Ms. Greenwood remarked.
"Burmese ancestry, I guess." She detached the kitten
from her sweater and held him at arm's length, looking
genuinely interested in Pumpkin for the first time since
Mandy had taken him out of her pouch.

Mandy felt a little more cheerful at the sight of the
kitten settling down in Ms. Greenwood's arms. Maybe if
no one claimed Pumpkin, Ms. Greenwood could take
him and look after him, like she looked after Cor and

Brock. *Except*, said a nagging voice in her head, *Ms. Greenwood doesn't like cats. Remember?*

"We found him at the Fox and Goose at lunchtime yesterday," she explained, resolutely pushing away any thoughts of matchmaking. "We think maybe he escaped from somewhere. But so far, no one in town can tell us a thing."

Ms. Greenwood frowned. "Did you find him around twelve o'clock? I seem to remember seeing a car waiting by the restaurant when I was in town. There was the sound of a car door opening and shutting, but no one got out. Then the car drove off. It was strange. If they were abandoning a kitten, it makes a little more sense. What do you think?"

Mandy closed her eyes as Ms. Greenwood's words sank in. It was suddenly horribly clear that Pumpkin wasn't lost at all. He had been deliberately abandoned — and a hundred posters weren't going to find an owner who didn't want to be found.

Mandy was very quiet as Dr. Adam drove them all back through the woods and into town. She kept thinking about what her dad had said back at Ms. Greenwood's house, about Pumpkin's owners. *They wouldn't be from around here, and having gone to the trouble of abandoning him, they certainly won't be taking him back.* She put her hand into her pocket and rested it on the sleeping kitten. It was a horrible feeling, knowing the friendly little cat was unwanted.

Dr. Adam had called the clinic from his cell phone, so Dr. Mason was expecting them.

In the examining room, Dr. Mason looked disbelievingly at James's ankle. "You say you only did this three hours ago?"

James nodded.

"There isn't much swelling," said the doctor with a frown. "I would have expected this whole area here to be bruised and puffy."

"Ms. Greenwood's comfrey and cabbage poultice must have helped," Mandy offered.

Dr. Mason's brow cleared. "Ah! Comfrey, the healer's favorite. That explains it." He cleaned James's ankle and bound it tightly with an elastic bandage. "You'll need crutches for a week or so," he continued, "but I'm not very concerned."

"Crutches!" James said in dismay. "But I'm going to the Halloween party as Harry Potter! I'll look really stupid."

Dr. Mason produced a pair of crutches from a tall closet beside his desk. "Better to be safe than sorry," he said, passing the crutches to James.

James rolled his eyes and reluctantly took the crutches from the doctor's hands.

"How about making them part of your costume?" John suggested.

"How?" James scoffed, peering at the crutches in disgust. "By turning them into giant wands?"

"That's not a bad idea," Mandy said.

Pumpkin chose that moment to pop his head out of Mandy's pocket and yowl, as if in agreement with Mandy's suggestion.

"I've never had a kitten come to my office before," Dr. Mason remarked, bending down to take a good look at Pumpkin. "He looks like a cat I used to have. Smudge was his name. Lovely nature."

"Would you like him, Dr. Mason?" Mandy asked eagerly. "We need to find him a home."

Dr. Mason smiled and shook his head. "I'm afraid Jigsaw and Puzzle would never forgive me," he said.

Jigsaw and Puzzle were Dr. Mason's pet rats. Mandy sighed and sank back into her seat. It had been worth a try.

James was still looking at the crutches, considering how to make them part of his costume. "I could make them look like wands by wrapping them up with black crepe paper, I suppose," he said.

Mandy forced herself to stop thinking about the kitten. "You could wrap the tips in silver foil," she suggested. "It'll look great, James. Really original."

James stood up and made a few hops with the crutches tucked under his arms. "OK, they aren't too bad," he conceded. He hopped a little farther. "In fact, they're kind of cool. I'll be the most unusual Harry Potter Welford's ever seen, that's for sure!"

The next day, Mandy met John at the Fox and Goose. They were going to visit James at his house to see if his ankle was any better.

John produced a bag of candy corn as they walked through town. "I thought James might like some of this," he said.

Seeing the candy corn made Mandy think of Pumpkin. She sighed, wondering for the hundredth time what they were going to do with the kitten. She'd managed to persuade her parents to let her keep him a little longer, just until she could work out what to do about finding a home for him. But she knew she had to do something quickly.

"Thinking about Pumpkin?" said John, glancing at her.

Mandy nodded. "I can't think of anyone who might take him in," she said sadly. "I've found homes for so many cats that everyone in Welford's got one now. What am I going to do?"

"Did you hear from anyone who saw the posters yesterday?" John asked.

"No," said Mandy. "But I wasn't that surprised after what Ms. Greenwood told us about the car outside the Fox and Goose. When someone abandons a kitten, they don't usually call up and confess." She looked at John. "You don't want a cat, do you?"

"It's hard enough being separated from Brandy and Bertie when I'm away at school, without having a cat, too," John pointed out.

Mandy dug her hands deep into her pockets. "I guess you're right," she said glumly. "At this rate, I'm going to have to take Pumpkin to the Cat Rescue Center in Walton. They're really nice there and everything, but . . ." She trailed off.

"I know," John said sympathetically. "It's not the same as having a good home, is it? Cheer up, Mandy. I'm sure we'll work something out."

Ahead of them, a boy was riding a red bike up and down the road. Mandy frowned. "Isn't that Ms. Greenwood's bike?" she said, shading her eyes to get a better look.

"You'd know better than me," John said. "You're the one who rode it yesterday."

"It *is* Ms. Greenwood's," Mandy said slowly. "I'm sure

of it." A cold feeling swirled around in her stomach. "And that's Adam Poole riding it."

The tall boy she'd seen the previous day swung the bike around and yanked it up onto its rear wheel. There was a shout of encouragement from his friends, who were gathered around the pond again.

"How come he's got it?" John said, frowning.

"He must have taken it," said Mandy. "He must have gone to Ms. Greenwood's last night after we left, like he threatened. Oh, John! We've got to go and see if she's OK!"

"What about James?"

"James can wait," Mandy said urgently. "Ms. Greenwood can't. Come on!"

She started running down the road toward the woods, with John close behind her. Awful thoughts raced through her mind with every step. Was their new friend all right? What else had Adam Poole and his gang taken? She ran, full of terrified energy, hoping that Ms. Greenwood wasn't hurt and vowing that she'd never give Matt Burness the benefit of the doubt again.

Mandy's legs were almost giving out when she turned off the muddy path and stumbled up to the house. She burst into the living room, fearing the worst.

Araminta Greenwood was sitting by her fire, looking pale but calm. "Thought you might show up," she said abruptly. "Must say I'm glad you have. It's good to see a friendly face."

John ran into the house behind Mandy, red-faced and wheezing, and leaned against the door to get his breath back.

"Are you all right, Ms. Greenwood?" Mandy asked, holding her hands to her aching sides. "We saw Adam Poole riding your bike. We came as quickly as we could."

Ms. Greenwood waved her hand out the window. "They've made a mess of my garden," she said. "And I can't find Brock anywhere. But I'm all right. Not hurt or anything."

Mandy looked out the window and was dismayed to see that the neat beds of comfrey and willow herb, parsley, and rosemary had been dug up and the plants flung around as if there had been a small whirlwind. And Brock! When she thought of the injured badger hiding somewhere, scared and upset by Ms. Greenwood's night visitors, she felt dizzy with rage.

Ms. Greenwood poured Mandy and James two cups of chamomile tea. "Have some of this," she said. "It'll calm you down."

Drinking tea was the last thing Mandy felt like doing.

Instead, she wanted to run back to town and shake Adam Poole until his teeth fell out. But she took the mug and tried to calm down.

"John and I can help find Brock," she said. "And we'll help you clean up the yard, too. Oh, Ms. Greenwood, I'm so sorry this happened. I feel like it's my fault."

Araminta Greenwood shook her head. "Nonsense," she said. "Those boys wanted revenge after our little argument the other day. They'd have come whether you'd met them in town yesterday or not." She put her chamomile tea down. "Now let's see if we can find Brock. He couldn't have gone far."

Mandy was glad to have something to do to take her mind off Matt Burness and his friends. She and John scoured the yard, hunting behind the woodpile and under the hedges, but there was no sign of the badger. Mandy tried not to think about the dangers of the forest for an injured animal.

A young crow swooped down and landed clumsily in her path. Cocking its black head, it appeared to wink at her before shuffling from one foot to the other and flapping its wings noisily.

"You must be Cor," Mandy said in delight, forgetting her anxiety for a minute. She reached out her hand, but Cor shuffled backward, gave a harsh croak, and took off again, flapping hard to get off the ground. Mandy looked up to see the crow circling overhead, almost as if he was helping them search for the badger. He really was a very inept flier. She immediately felt more cheerful at the thought of an extra pair of eyes and turned back to the task.

But even with Cor's help, Brock was nowhere to be found.

"Did you look in here as well as outside, Ms. Greenwood?" John asked when he and Mandy went back inside.

The woman nodded. "Though my mind may not have been on it," she admitted. "Perhaps it's worth another look."

They all looked up as an odd shuffling sound came from a tall cupboard beside the stove.

Ms. Greenwood's brow cleared. "He's in the pantry!" she exclaimed.

Mandy ran over and gently pulled the door open. At first she couldn't see anything in the darkness. But after a few moments she made out a striped snout, covered with cookie crumbs.

"How did he ever get in there?" asked Araminta Greenwood, perplexed. "I haven't been in there since yesterday."

"It must have closed after him," John guessed.

"Maybe he never even saw the vandals. Maybe he just got locked in!"

Brock blinked at them all before returning to the cookies scattered on the floor.

Mandy laughed with relief. "What a smart badger," she said. "If you're going to get locked in anywhere, where could be better than a cupboard full of food?"

Nine

The next morning dawned bright and frosty. Perched on a stool in the kitchen, Mandy reached across the table and selected an apple from the fruit bowl. Pumpkin was sleeping peacefully in her lap, tired out after an energetic game of chasing his tail. Looking down at him, Mandy felt her heart ache. He trusted her to find him a new home, and she knew she was letting him down.

"When's Ms. Greenwood coming to borrow your bike, Mom?" she asked.

"She was going to call from town this morning," replied Dr. Emily, checking her watch. "She'll probably be here soon. I can't believe those boys stole her bike and she didn't report it!"

Mandy crunched into her apple. "She said she didn't want to involve the police," she explained between mouthfuls. "We made her promise to get a cell phone, though. She was going to get one in Walton today, so she can call us if anything like that ever happens again."

"I'm sure James was sorry to miss all the drama," Dr. Emily commented.

"He was," Mandy replied. "But I called him last night and told him everything."

"Poor Ms. Greenwood," Dr. Emily said, and sighed. "Those boys need to be taught a lesson, picking on an elderly woman that way." She glanced at Mandy and frowned. "Don't eat any more apples, Mandy. Those are for tonight's apple bobbing!"

"Sorry." Mandy blushed and put the second apple back in the bowl. "I wasn't thinking."

Dr. Emily took her white coat down from its peg and put it on. "And on the subject of thinking," she said, looking meaningfully at Pumpkin.

"I know," Mandy said guiltily. "I'm going to take him around town today and show him off. The personal touch always works better than just a poster. Someone's going to want him." She said this with more conviction than she felt.

"Well, I hope they do," Dr. Emily replied as kindly as she could. "But if you can't find anyone today, then we have to take Pumpkin to the Cat Rescue Center first thing tomorrow. Understood?"

Mandy nodded reluctantly, feeling very glum. She had been successful in the past finding homes for animals, especially cats, but it looked as if this was going to be her first failure. She gently put the sleeping kitten down on his cushion and followed her mother into the waiting room.

Mrs. Ponsonby looked up as they entered. "Dr. Emily!" she exclaimed. "Pandora's toenail is much better, thanks to your husband's marvelous ministrations the other day."

Dr. Emily smiled. "I'm so glad, Mrs. Ponsonby. We'll take a look under that dressing in just a moment and see if it needs changing."

"Excuse me, Dr. Emily," said Jean, looking up from the appointment book. "I have a message here for you. Now, where did I put it?"

Mandy and her mother waited patiently as Jean hunted around for her notepad. Jean was famous for losing things — the appointment book had been found two days earlier underneath a pile of flea-prevention pamphlets.

"Ah, here it is." Jean adjusted her glasses. "Ms. Green-

wood called from the phone booth to say she'd arrive at
eight-thirty. She should be here any moment."

"Ms. Greenwood again," said Mrs. Ponsonby with a
sniff. "I would advise you to have nothing more to do
with that strange woman, Dr. Emily. I heard those awful, screeching noises near her cottage again the other
day. It sounded like" — she lowered her voice — "like
some poor creature being *tortured.*"

Mandy was about to explain about Cor when all at
once a familiar screech filled the air.

"Oh!" Mrs. Ponsonby squeaked in horror. "That's the
noise! That's the awful noise I heard in the woods!"

Ms. Greenwood filled the door of the clinic. Her cape
swirled around her orange-and-black-striped legs, and
Cor the crow was sitting on her shoulder.

"Ms. Greenwood! You've brought Cor!" Mandy exclaimed in delight.

"He didn't want to be left behind," Ms. Greenwood
explained. "I hope he won't make a nuisance of himself."

Pandora the Peke gave a frightened yelp at the sight
of the black crow. Mrs. Ponsonby glared at Ms. Greenwood. "Your bird is frightening my poor girl," she said
imperiously.

Cor cocked his head to one side and made a chirping
noise. Pandora stopped yelping and began to look in-

terested instead. Then she gave a sharp yip and tipped her head playfully to one side. Mrs. Ponsonby's words died on her lips as Cor chirped again and Pandora yipped back. It looked for all the world as though the two animals were having a conversation.

Mrs. Ponsonby found her voice at last. "W-well," she stuttered. "Well, I . . . Goodness me, they seem to like each other!"

"Cor's a friendly fellow," Ms. Greenwood said, smiling. "When you get to know him."

Mrs. Ponsonby gave the woman a curious look, half ashamed and half impressed. Pandora squirmed in Mrs. Ponsonby's arms as Cor fluffed out his wings and looked pleased with himself.

Harmony at Animal Ark, Mandy thought happily.

Out of the corner of her eye, she saw an apple roll slowly through the door to the kitchen. Half a second later, Pumpkin flew after it, paws outstretched and whiskers quivering. Pandora jumped out of Mrs. Ponsonby's arms in a frenzy of barking as soon as she saw the kitten, which made Cor screech and fly up into the air, wings flapping madly.

Dr. Emily bent down and picked up the mischievous kitten. "We have to find you a new home before you drive us all crazy!" she said, and chuckled.

Mandy couldn't bring herself to join in the laughter. A new home for Pumpkin still felt as far away as the moon.

After morning clinic hours, Mandy tucked Pumpkin into her sweatshirt pouch, put on her jacket, and went outside to meet John. They walked happily down the road to Lilac Cottage, where Mandy's grandparents lived.

Dorothy and Tom Hope were delighted to see them. After a cup of hot chocolate and several of Dorothy's homemade ginger cookies, Mandy took a deep breath, put her hand into her pocket, and pulled out Pumpkin. The kitten promptly woke up with a vigorous shake of his head.

"Oh, you've brought that sweet little kitten!" Mandy's grandmother exclaimed. "Imagine taking him on a walk with you!"

"It's not exactly a walk," Mandy replied, trying to choose her words carefully. "You see, we need to find Pumpkin a home, so I thought we'd take him around town and see if anyone wanted him."

Tom Hope picked up the kitten in his big hands and cradled him there for a moment. He glanced at Mandy, understanding in his eyes. "And you hoped maybe we'd consider it?"

"Would you?" Mandy said, her words suddenly tumbling out in a rush. "He'd be no trouble. Well," she amended, "all kittens are a bit of trouble, but it would be worth it, don't you think? I'd love it if he went to someone in the family."

Pumpkin yawned so widely that they were given a full view of his pink, ridged mouth and delicate tongue. Dorothy Hope laughed and looked across at her husband. "He is very sweet, Tom," she said. "Do you think that maybe we could?"

Tom Hope put Pumpkin down on the sofa, where the

kitten immediately attacked a tassel on a cushion. Within moments the tassel was torn to shreds, bits of silk thread strewn across the sofa.

"He certainly has a taste for your cushions," Mandy's grandfather observed humorously. "Yes, I suppose we could consider it."

Mandy half rose from her seat in delight, but her grandfather put his hand in the air. "But there is someone we have to ask first," he said. "Smoky may have a very different opinion on the subject. And we have to be fair, Mandy. Smoky was here first."

On cue, Smoky stalked into the living room and spotted the kitten. Mandy held her breath as the older cat's tail began to bristle. *Oh, Smoky, please give Pumpkin a chance,* she thought, crossing her fingers as tightly as she could.

Smoky started growling at the back of his throat and stepped stiffly toward the kitten. Pumpkin yowled with fright and backed deep into the sofa cushions. Smoky continued growling, his eyes fixed on the kitten. When Mandy's grandfather picked Pumpkin up and put him on the floor in front of Smoky, the older cat's growling got louder. Pumpkin batted a tentative paw, inviting Smoky to play. But Smoky only narrowed his eyes and angrily twitched his tail.

Pumpkin pounced in an instant and latched onto

Smoky's tail. With a yowl of outrage, Smoky lashed out with his claws, making Pumpkin shoot under the sofa in terror.

Dorothy Hope met Mandy's eyes. "It won't work, dear," she said, bending down to pick up Smoky. "Your grandpa's right. Smoky was here first. It just wouldn't be fair to make him share his home with another cat. I'm so sorry."

John had managed to coax Pumpkin out from beneath the sofa and was now trying to soothe the frightened kitten.

Mandy felt crushed with disappointment. "I understand," she said, standing up. "Thanks for considering it. And thanks for the cookies, Gran."

Walking back into the center of Welford with John, she realized just how much she had been counting on her grandparents to adopt the kitten. She couldn't think of a single other person who might take Pumpkin in. The situation was getting desperate.

Pumpkin was half inside the neck of John's sweatshirt, his face peeking out over the top. It would have made Mandy laugh if she'd been in a better mood. "Let's go and see James," John suggested. "He needs cheering up, and so do we. And you never know. Together we might think of something."

*   *   *

"About time!" James exclaimed, looking up from a mound of black crepe paper and glitter when Mandy put her head around the kitchen door. "I thought you were never coming." He gestured at the crepe paper. "I've been decorating my crutches. What do you think?"

Pumpkin wriggled out of John's sweatshirt and took a flying leap into the crunchy crepe paper, where he landed with a springy-sounding thump. Like Ms. Greenwood and her cape in the woods two nights earlier, he was almost perfectly camouflaged in the paper, only his bright orange eyes giving him away.

Soon Pumpkin was clowning around, playing with the edges of the paper with his sharp little teeth and making them all laugh. *It's hard to feel worried with that kitten around,* Mandy thought, breathless from trying to catch the tumbling scrap of black fur. She knew they should be planning what to do with Pumpkin, but her mood had lifted so much that she felt completely confident everything was going to work out just fine.

Blackie trotted in from the kitchen to investigate the noise. He took one look at Pumpkin and barked eagerly, leaping forward to play. Caught off guard, Pumpkin tumbled helplessly onto his back. John grabbed Blackie's collar and pulled him backward just in time as Pumpkin scrambled back onto his paws. Mandy picked the kitten up and cuddled him, whispering soothing words.

Sheepishly, James took Blackie from John. "Sorry, guys," he apologized. "Blackie doesn't realize how big he is. He was only trying to play."

Mandy planted one more kiss on Pumpkin's head and tucked him safely into her pouch. "I'm sure Pumpkin wanted to play, too," she said. "He reminds me of a puppy sometimes, the way he wants to join in with everything. Don't worry about it, James. It's probably time for us to keep on walking, anyway."

"May I come?" James asked hopefully. "Blackie could use the walk, and I need to practice on my crutches."

Mandy reached over and punched her friend gently on the arm. "You don't have to ask!" she said. "Of course you may. We have to go to the store at the post office to pick up supplies for tonight's party. We could use an extra pair of hands, even if they do have crutches attached!"

Mr. McFarlane had already put the Hopes' party order into several shopping bags by the time they got to the post office, so all Mandy had to do was arrange who was going to carry what.

"James, you take the heavy ones — the lemonade and fruit juices," she instructed. "We can loop the bags over your crutch handles. That will save them from cutting into your hands."

James tried hopping across the shop with the shopping bags and found that the best method was to swing the crutches a little more than usual. He picked up speed as he neared the door and managed to stop just before cannoning into a stack of baked beans.

"You'll fizz up the soft drinks if you do that too much," Mr. McFarlane warned.

James hastily dragged his laden crutches out of the way as the post office door gave its familiar tinkle and swung open to reveal Araminta Greenwood. She was looking extremely agitated.

"Mandy!" Ms. Greenwood looked relieved to see her. "I — oh, dear."

Mandy guessed in an instant that the boys had returned to the house in the woods. She was alarmed to see Araminta Greenwood sway very slightly. Mr. McFarlane pulled a chair out from behind the counter so she could sit down.

Mandy knelt down beside her. "What happened this time?"

"An overturned garbage can," said Ms. Greenwood with a shake of her head. "It's a little thing, I know, but . . . Well, it did scare me."

Mandy felt furious. "That's enough!" she cried fiercely. "We can't let those boys do this anymore!"

Deep inside Mandy's pocket, Pumpkin gave an extremely loud and eerie yowl of displeasure.

"Oh!" Mr. McFarlane clutched at his chest, his eyes wide and shocked as he looked around the store. "What in the world was that?"

Mandy brought Pumpkin out of her pocket. "He's the one on the poster in your window, Mr. McFarlane," she said, trying to bring her temper under control so she wouldn't frighten the kitten. "We're trying to find a home for him."

"A home!" Mr. McFarlane echoed, staring at the kitten in disbelief. "That animal sounds like he should be out in the jungle! His meow is enough to frighten the daylights out of anyone — particularly at Halloween."

There was a pause. Suddenly, Mandy's eyes were full of fire.

"I've just had the most fantastic idea!" she said. "I know how to stop those boys from bothering Ms. Greenwood. It's Halloween. Why don't we give them the fright of their lives?"

Ten

At five-thirty that afternoon, Mandy stood by the fire in Ms. Greenwood's house and adjusted her Halloween mask. It was time for Operation Howl. If everything went according to plan, Matt Burness and his friends would never bother Ms. Greenwood again.

"Your mask looks fantastic," John said approvingly. "When those boys see you in the woods, they'll think they've gone crazy!"

"Tell me," said Araminta Greenwood as she adjusted the back of John's ghostly white sheet, "is this luminous paint?"

"Yes, it is," John replied. "I'll glow in the dark. And if that doesn't frighten them, I don't know what will."

James twitched unhappily at his cape. "I'm sure my crutches are going to get in the way," he grumbled. "It's not very scary, is it, to see someone limping toward you?"

Mandy tightened her cat tail and stroked back her long black whiskers. She felt calm and excited at the same time. "That's where you're wrong, James," she said. "Imagine hearing not just two thumps approaching you in the dark, but *three* — a foot and two crutches! We'll scare those vandals out of their socks!"

She bent down and gave Blackie an encouraging pat. "And you look very batlike, Blackie," she said happily. "You'll be terrifying."

The black Labrador did look faintly batlike in his red luminous collar. With his glossy black coat, the rest of him would blend in beautifully with the trees.

"Are you sure you aren't missing your Halloween party?" Araminta Greenwood asked.

"We'll be back in plenty of time for the party," Mandy assured her. "It doesn't start for an hour and a half. This is much more important."

"What if the vandals don't come back tonight?" said John.

Mandy smiled. "Of course they'll come back. It's Halloween! They won't be able to resist trying to spook Ms. Greenwood on the scariest night of the year. Now, what props have you brought?"

John dug around in his backpack. "A CD of sound effects," he announced. "I borrowed it from my dad. Sometimes there are theme nights at the restaurant, you know? It's got some fantastic stuff on it — howling wind, baying wolves, creaky doors." He fished a little deeper into his bag. "And here's the CD player," he went on. "We'll put the speakers up in the branch of a tree, and I'll use the remote control to switch it on. It'll be great."

James held out a large jar full of green slime. Mandy made a face. "Ugh. What's that?"

"Green gunk," James explained. "It's my own recipe. We'll daub it around the gate and the fence. Wait till they put their hands in it!" he added.

"Excellent," Mandy said with satisfaction. "I've brought some cobweb spray that we can string across the trees. And I have Pumpkin, too, of course." She patted her sweatshirt pouch. "Get that meow ready, Pumpkin," she instructed. "Tonight's your big night."

She waited for the kitten to meow in response, but there was no sound from her pouch. Mandy carefully drew the kitten out and held him up close to her face. Pumpkin's nose stayed where it was, tucked beneath his tail.

"Is he all right?" James asked, leaning forward.

Mandy tickled Pumpkin's chin. "Hey, little fellow!" she said encouragingly. "What's up?"

Pumpkin sat up slowly in Mandy's hand and blinked at her. Then he yowled softly and tragically. It was the saddest thing Mandy had ever heard, and she realized for the first time that he must be feeling lonely, with no other animals to play with and no home except for a cage in the clinic's residential unit and a cushion on the kitchen table.

"He needs his mother," Ms. Greenwood said. "Youngster like that. Can't be right for him, having no home."

"I know," Mandy replied unhappily. "It's not fair, always carrying him around like a shopping bag. I'm trying my best to find him a home, Ms. Greenwood, but I'm not doing very well."

"He'll be fine," Ms. Greenwood said abruptly. "Bright spark like that. He'll make his home where he pleases."

I just hope he's not too sad to yowl for us tonight, Mandy thought miserably, tucking the kitten back into her pouch.

"I have something I would like to add to these sound effects of yours, by the way," said Ms. Greenwood as she walked with them down to the gate. She gave a sharp whistle, and Cor fluttered out of nowhere to land on her arm. "I can't guarantee that Cor will join in, but I hope that he will," she said.

Mandy was thrilled. "May I pet him?"

"Of course," said Ms. Greenwood. "He'd like that."

The crow seemed to enjoy the feel of Mandy petting his dusty black feathers and made soft croaking noises in the back of his throat, almost like a cat purring.

"Time is moving on," Ms. Greenwood reminded them. "Let's get everything in place and hope that our visitors don't arrive too soon!"

Setting up the props took longer than Mandy thought. She was acutely aware of every rustle out in the woods, but this time it wasn't because she was scared of ghosts. If the boys came too early, the whole thing would be ruined.

But they were in luck. When everything was in place, Araminta Greenwood folded her arms and looked at them. "I am not good at saying thank you," she said abruptly. "And I should probably discourage what's about to happen here. But I can't help thinking that this will be a much better way of getting the message across to my visitors than a trip to the police station in a thrilling police car." She smiled. "So thank you," she said. "And good luck." Then she turned around and strode back to the house.

Mandy, James, and John crouched down behind the

trees and began to wait. The minutes ticked away, and Mandy felt her first twinge of doubt. What if John was right? What if the boys never came? What if Pumpkin didn't yowl? She petted the kitten and bit her thumbnail anxiously, staring hard into the night.

Click, click, click. It was the unmistakable sound of bicycle wheel spokes, turning very slowly over the ruts and bumps of the woods. Mandy tensed as she heard voices.

". . . might be expecting us after last night," Adam Poole was saying in a low voice. "So keep quiet, OK?"

Peering around the base of her tree, Mandy watched as Adam Poole, Ben Stevens, Liam Collins, and Matt Burness crept up to the gate.

Adam Poole propped the bike up against the fence and smiled at his gang. "Liam, you dig up a few more of the witch's herbs. Ben, the witch's woodpile needs a little rearranging. And you, country boy," he whispered, turning to Matt Burness, "let's see if you have the guts to use this." He thrust what looked like a can of spray paint at Matt. Then he puffed out his chest and looked important. "And this little gate will do for me. Not really built to keep out the ghosties and goblins. Time it came off its puny little hinges — *eurghgh!*"

He snatched his hand off the gate in disgust and stared at the sticky mess on his fingers. Mandy nearly burst out laughing. She turned and nodded at John, who aimed his remote control at the tree just beside Liam Collins.

"*Whshooshwhshoosh* . . . The sound of a spooky wind on a lonely moor began to fill the air.

Adam Poole snapped his head around, still holding his green-gunked hand up in the air.

"*Arooooo!*" bayed a very large, very hungry wolf.

"Wolves!" Ben Stevens said and gasped, spinning around.

"In Welford?" Adam Poole scoffed, looking extremely uncertain. "Nah. Just . . . just the wind or something."

The sound of an enormous door began creaking open, slowly, horrifyingly. . . .

"I don't like this!" Liam Collins whimpered, backing straight into a line of sticky cobweb spray. He gave a shriek and frantically tried to pull the cobwebs off his neck.

Mandy raised her arm. It was the signal! The boys yelled in terror as four *things* rushed out of the trees toward them: a giant cat, a luminous ghost, a swirling cape, and an odd red stripe that seemed to bound through midair.

Craaaa! Right on cue, Cor flapped clumsily over the boys' heads and screeched. Mandy pulled Pumpkin out of her sweatshirt and held him high in the air.

Now's your moment, Pumpkin! she thought, desperately willing him to meow. *Yowl now, and I promise I'll find you the best home in the world!*

And the kitten, thoroughly overexcited by the commotion, gave the most terrific yowl of his life.

Yaiiiieeeeeoooooowwwaarrrr!

Adam Poole wheeled around and blundered off into the woods, screaming his head off. Ben Stevens and Liam Collins crashed into each other, skidded in a puddle of green gunk, and fell flat on their faces. Shrieking and yelling, they scrambled to their feet as fast as they could and fled toward the path. But Matt Burness appeared to be frozen to the spot, staring in horror at a quaking bush just beside the gate.

Tucking Pumpkin back into her sweatshirt pocket, Mandy skidded to a halt. A quaking bush? That wasn't one of their tricks. James and John raced up to Mandy, breathing hard. They all stared at the bush in alarm. What was in there?

Matt looked around at them, his eyes huge. He didn't seem surprised to see that the four phantoms had turned into Mandy, James, John, and Blackie. He didn't even seem able to speak. He just pointed.

The bush rustled and shook like a living thing. Mandy's heart was in her throat. So far, everything had been a great laugh. But it *was* Halloween. And this . . .

this was unexplained, impossible — and totally the scariest thing she'd ever seen in her life. She squeezed Pumpkin so hard that the kitten mewed and wriggled in protest.

"What's in there?" John whispered, clutching onto Mandy's arm.

"I don't k-k-know," Mandy stammered. She glanced at Ms. Greenwood's house. How long would it take them to run to safety there before the . . . the thing in the bush *attacked* them?

The leaves at the bottom of the bush parted, and a long, pointed snout appeared. There was another frantic rustle, and it was followed by a broad set of shoulders and a thickly furred black-and-white back. Brock the badger emerged from underneath the bush and shook his head. He stared up at his astounded audience.

Mandy found her voice. "It's Brock!" she croaked. She began to laugh with relief. "It's just Brock!"

Blackie stepped forward and sniffed cautiously at the badger. Brock growled a grumpy warning and began to shuffle away, under the gate and up the path toward the house.

"Was that a badger?" Matt Burness sounded amazed.

Mandy nodded.

"Cool!" Matt whispered.

They all stared at one another, realizing at the same moment how odd the situation was. There was an embarrassed silence, and Mandy felt confused. *Matt Burness is the enemy*, she thought. *Isn't he?*

"Good trick," Matt said at last, gesturing at their costumes. "The, er, wind and creaky door and stuff. How did you do that?" He sounded genuinely curious.

"Sound effects CD," John replied warily.

"It was great," Matt said. "Adam nearly collapsed."

Suddenly, they were all laughing at the memory of Adam Poole rushing off in terror, and hostilities were somehow forgotten.

"I always knew you were all right," Mandy told Matt, with a glance at James. "Anyone with a dog like Biscuit is bound to be OK."

Matt smiled shyly.

"Listen," John said, "why don't you come up to the house? It's getting cold out here."

Matt took a fast step backward. "With the witch? No way!"

"Yes, way," James said firmly. "You owe her an explanation. And an apology."

"You have to face Ms. Greenwood sometime," Mandy pointed out.

"But she'll turn me into something!" Matt insisted, looking fearful.

"Don't be dense," James scoffed. "She's not a witch. She's just a wise woman who lives in the woods."

Mandy rolled her eyes. "It's about time you figured that out, James."

James shrugged. "I've known all along," he replied casually. "I was just teasing you."

The front door of the house flew open, and a wide stripe of golden light flooded the yard. Ms. Greenwood was silhouetted on the doorstep, her arms folded and her shadow long and witchy on the path to the door.

"You caught one of the visitors, I see," she said icily. "Now, what are we going to do with him?"

Mandy watched Matt's reaction. At first, the red-headed boy seemed too scared to say or do anything. Then, rather awkwardly, he bent down, picked up Ms. Greenwood's bike, and leaned it safely against the fence. It was clearly a gesture of peace.

Araminta Greenwood regarded Matt in silence for a minute or two. Matt squirmed beneath her gaze and shivered.

"Are you cold?" the woman asked.

Matt nodded, shading his eyes from the light.

"No more than you deserve," Ms. Greenwood said severely. "Now, do I get an apology, or do we stand here all night?"

Matt shuffled his feet. "Sorry," he whispered.

Mandy, James, and John ushered Matt up the path and into the house. Blinking in the light, he looked around the little room uncertainly.

"Sit down," said Ms. Greenwood. "You've had a scare. A well-deserved one in your case, young man, but a scare nonetheless." She picked up the large teapot on the stove and poured out four cups of fragrant, yellowish tea. "Chamomile," she said. "Calms the nerves. Drink up, all of you."

Soon they were all sipping the warming tea. Mandy petted Pumpkin, who was fast asleep on her lap, and hunted around for something to say. She looked at the silent, subdued-looking Matt, and said the first thing that came into her head.

"How's Biscuit?"

Matt's eyes lit up. "He's fantastic," he said right away.

"How long have you had him?" James asked.

Suddenly, Matt started talking. He explained how his dad had bought Biscuit for the whole family, to help them adjust to moving to the country. "We always wanted a dog in Walton, but Mom never let us have one." He told them about how worried he'd been about leaving all his friends and how he was sure he'd never find any new ones. "Adam Poole and that gang were better than no friends at all," he said, sounding apologetic.

Mandy leaned forward. "And do you still feel the same way about Adam Poole?" she prompted.

Matt looked down at his hands. "He's not a friend," he said. "I don't know why I didn't see it in the first place. I've made a real mess of things, haven't I?"

Ms. Greenwood nodded. "You certainly have," she said. "But the damage doesn't have to be permanent."

"I'll help you clean up the mess in the yard," Matt promised. "And I'll clean your bike, too. I'm sorry, Ms. Greenwood. I really am."

"Good," said the woman. "In the meantime, can you promise me that those ex-friends of yours won't be returning to Welford?"

"They only came because I invited them," said Matt. "They kept on saying how boring it was here. I'm sure they won't come anymore." He looked sad for a minute. "So I really am friendless now, I guess."

Mandy smiled at him. "I wouldn't say that," she said.

Suddenly, she felt Pumpkin's small claws digging into her legs. The kitten had woken up again. "We'd almost forgotten about you!" she said, scooping up the kitten and kissing him on the nose. "You were a star tonight, Pumpkin. I'm sure that yowl was the final straw."

Pumpkin stretched and yowled obligingly, and Matt's eyes widened. "I thought you said you used sound effects!" he exclaimed.

"Pumpkin was one of them." James said. He grinned, as the kitten started sharpening his claws on Mandy's knee.

"He's very cute." Matt reached out and tickled the kitten on the head.

"I don't suppose you want a cat?" Mandy asked hopefully.

Matt shook his head. "Sorry. My mom's allergic. Is he looking for a home?"

"Yes." Mandy sighed. "And tonight's my last chance."

Cor stuck his head around the side of the sofa and made them all jump. Pumpkin sat up and regarded the large black bird with interest. Raising a paw, he batted it in the crow's direction. Cor's head retreated into his shoulders, and he clicked his beak warningly. Taking no notice, Pumpkin jumped off Mandy's knee and bounced over to the crow, wagging his tail and preparing to pounce.

Craaa! Cor screeched and flapped his wings. The kitten leaped sideways in fright, stuck his claws into Ms. Greenwood's orange-and-black-striped tights, and shinnied up the surprised woman as if she were a drainpipe.

"Steady there, little cat!" Ms. Greenwood exclaimed, reaching awkwardly for the kitten as he tried to burrow into her black sweater. "There's nothing to be scared of.

Remember what I told you about not bothering badgers? Well, the same applies to crows."

All at once, Mandy noticed two things. First, there was a kind of *rightness* to seeing Pumpkin in Ms. Greenwood's arms, tonight of all nights — the good witch and her familiar, together at Halloween. And second, with his black fur and orange eyes, Pumpkin looked as if he was made to match Ms. Greenwood's tights.

"Ms. Greenwood?" she said hesitantly. "I know you said you don't like cats and everything, but Pumpkin's got Burmese in him so he's really sociable and friendly and more like a dog anyway, and . . ." She shook her head impatiently at the muddle she was making of this. "What I'm trying to say is, well, Pumpkin really likes you, and I think you'd be perfect together. Would you consider giving him a home, please? He just looks like he's *made* to be with you."

Ms. Greenwood took a long, hard look at the kitten in her arms. Pumpkin wriggled, put out his tiny pink tongue, and started vigorously washing the elderly woman's thumb. Ms. Greenwood laughed out loud for the first time since Mandy had met her. Then she nodded, very slowly. "I think that perhaps you were right about finding a cat to suit me, Mandy," she said. "This kitten's a handful, but between us, Brock, Cor, and I will keep him in his place. Yes, he can live with us. We'll be pleased to have him."

Mandy jumped up and hugged Pumpkin and his new mistress. "That's perfect!" she exclaimed, beside herself with delight. "Just perfect!"

"Hey, look at the time!" John exclaimed suddenly. "It's five to seven. The party's going to start without us!"

Mandy swung around, looking horrified. "Oh, no! What's Mom going to say?"

"I have an idea," said Ms. Greenwood, reaching for her new cell phone. "Why don't I call your parents and invite them here instead?"

"Here in the woods?" James asked, sounding excited. "Wow! How spooky would that be?"

"It would be a pity to waste good cobweb spray," John pointed out. "And the sound effects are still up in the tree."

The evening was just getting better and better, Mandy decided. "That's your best idea yet, Ms. Greenwood," she said happily.

*   *   *

Mandy's parents were there within twenty minutes, with the bags of chips and the soft drinks. Tom and Dorothy Hope came ten minutes later, bringing with them Walter Pickard and Ernie Bell. Mandy's grandfather had somehow attached a small rubber spider to his mustache — "Just following the instructions on the invitation, Mandy!" — and her gran was wearing a splendid black witch's hat.

"We were with your grandparents when Ms. Greenwood called. She was kind enough to invite us, too," Ernie Bell explained, looking impressed at the sight of Cor perching on the back of the sofa.

"We were sorry to miss your costumes at the trick-or-treating earlier," Walter explained, grinning at the sight of the pumpkins on Ms. Greenwood's windowsill. "And I did always love a good Halloween party."

James's parents couldn't come, but John's dad popped in to say hello, apologizing that he wasn't able to stay for long. "It's a busy night at the restaurant," he explained.

"Did you bring the rest of the candy corn, Dad?" John asked.

His dad put his hands up. "Sorry. We gave it all away to the trick-or-treaters. It was very popular — even without kittens in it!"

Mandy grabbed John's arm and pulled him away. "Never mind. We have lots for the games. Come on, let's set them up!"

Ms. Greenwood had invited Matt's parents as well, so the little house was full of people enjoying themselves by eight o'clock. Matt took over as DJ and was extremely good at it, mixing Mandy's dance CDs with John's spooky sound effects. The slimy things in jars made Mandy scream, and Walter got covered in sugar from the doughnuts hanging on strings. Mandy's dad, meanwhile, won the cookie race.

"It's my diet," he laughed, putting his arm round Mandy's mom. "Sheer hunger drove me on!" He winked at Mandy, and she wondered if he'd been secretly practicing.

Pumpkin had cheered up immensely since his argument with Cor and wanted to join in everything: chasing Mandy's cat tail, batting pieces of candy corn through the powdered sugar, and swinging from the hanging cookies like a small furry monkey. Mandy watched him fondly. *It's as if he knows that he's come home*, she thought. Ms. Greenwood had already given him a saucer of milk and promised Mandy that she would keep Pumpkin in her bedroom at night so that he was safely out of Brock's and Cor's way. Food, love, and a bed for the night. What more could a kitten want?

The last game was bobbing for apples. Mandy and Ms. Greenwood were just about to duck for the one remaining apple when suddenly —

SPLASH!

Pumpkin fell from an overhead cookie string, straight into the water.

"There's never going to be a dull moment with Pumpkin around, Ms. Greenwood," Mandy said, gasping and wiping her face.

The elderly woman's eyes gleamed. "Who likes dull moments?" she replied. "Come on, Mandy. Race you to the last apple!"

ANIMAL ARK
Where animals come first

Read all the Animal Ark books!

by Ben M. Baglio

$3.99 Each!

❏ 0-439-09700-2	**Bunnies in the Bathroom**		❏ 0-439-09698-7	**Kitten in the Cold**
❏ 0-439-34407-7	**Cat in a Crypt**		❏ 0-590-18749-X	**Kittens in the Kitchen**
❏ 0-439-34393-3	**Cats at the Campground**		❏ 0-439-34392-5	**Mare in the Meadow**
❏ 0-439-34413-1	**Colt in the Cave**		❏ 0-590-66231-7	**Ponies at the Point**
❏ 0-439-34386-0	**Dog at the Door**		❏ 0-439-34388-7	**Pony in a Package**
❏ 0-439-34408-5	**Dog in the Dungeon**		❏ 0-590-18750-3	**Pony on the Porch**
❏ 0-439-23021-7	**Dolphin in the Deep**		❏ 0-439-34391-7	**Pup at the Palace**
❏ 0-439-34415-8	**Foal in the Fog**		❏ 0-590-18751-1	**Puppies in the Pantry**
❏ 0-439-34385-2	**Foals in the Field**		❏ 0-439-34389-5	**Puppy in a Puddle**
❏ 0-439-23018-7	**Guinea Pig in the Garage**		❏ 0-439-68496-X	**Racehorse in the Rain**
❏ 0-439-09701-0	**Hamster in a Handbasket**		❏ 0-590-18757-0	**Sheepdog in the Snow**
❏ 0-439-44893-X	**Hamster in the Holly**		❏ 0-439-68757-8	**Siamese in the Sun**
❏ 0-439-34387-9	**Horse in the House**		❏ 0-439-34126-4	**Stallion in the Storm**
❏ 0-439-44891-3	**Hound at the Hospital**		❏ 0-439-34390-9	**Tabby in the Tub**
❏ 0-439-44897-2	**Hound on the Heath**		❏ 0-439-44892-1	**Terrier in the Tinsel**
❏ 0-439-44894-8	**Husky in a Hut**			

Available wherever you buy books, or use this order form.

Scholastic Inc., P.O. Box 7502, Jefferson City, MO 65102

Please send me the books I have checked above. I am enclosing $_____ (please add $2.00 to cover shipping and handling). Send check or money order—no cash or C.O.D.s please.

Name_____Age_____

Address_____

City_____State/Zip_____

Please allow four to six weeks for delivery. Offer good in the U.S. only. Sorry, mail orders are not available to residents of Canada. Prices subject to change.

◤ SCHOLASTIC

SCHOLASTIC and associated logos are trademarks and/or registered trademarks of Scholastic Inc.

ABBL0706